CHAOS RISING

AN EDGE OF COLLAPSE PREQUEL

KYLA STONE

PAPER MOON PRESS

Chaos Rising

Printed in the United States of America

Cover design by Christian Bentulan

Book formatting by Vellum

First Printed in 2019

ISBN: 978-1-945410-45-1

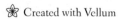 Created with Vellum

1

If Liam Coleman had known this day would end in disaster, destruction, and death, he never would have left his isolated homestead in northwest Michigan.

But he was here, stuck in the cold and bluster and crowds outside of O'Hare International airport in Chicago. It was Christmas Eve morning and everywhere he looked, people hustled past him, bright holiday sweaters beneath their heavy coats. The airport shops and restaurants were decorated in gaudy lights, shiny tinsel, and fake trees covered in overpriced souvenir ornaments.

Liam was only doing this for his twin brother, whom he hadn't seen in four years. In forty-eight hours, he'd be back on a plane headed for the peace and solitude he craved.

The sky was gray and thick with heavy clouds. Cold air stung his exposed cheeks and neck. He flipped up the collar of his fur-lined parka, pressed his gray knit beanie over his ears, and readjusted his backpack. His suitcase pressed against his left leg.

Someone bumped into his elbow as they jostled for a spot at the crowded curb, everyone waiting for rides from taxis, Uber, or loved ones. Hundreds of cars honked and braked and rolled slowly past, their tires spitting up dirty chunks of snow and ice.

Liam hated crowds.

If his brother didn't show in five minutes, he was calling an Uber. Or screw it. He'd just walk. He'd probably make the twenty-five miles to their apartment faster than it'd take to drive in this traffic.

He scanned the clumps and clusters of people—business folks standing apart with briefcases, buttoned coats, and tense faces; harried parents with shivering children swirling around their legs; college-aged kids eager for a holiday adventure in the big city.

No one suspicious. No one out of place. Still, his anxiety remained elevated. His Gerber MK II tactical knife and gun case were packed in his suitcase. He hated not having the knife on him. He hated not having his Glock 19 holstered comfortably at his side even more.

He shifted his gaze to the traffic lanes again and spotted Lincoln's cherry-red Audi A4. A few freezing minutes later, his brother managed to squeeze into a slot by the curb and popped the trunk.

"Look who it is!" Lincoln buzzed down the passenger window from the driver's seat, leaning over the center console and waving enthusiastically. "Get the hell inside where it's warm!"

The familiar sound of his brother's voice warmed him, but regret swiftly followed. Against his will, his throat tightened.

Lincoln's wife, Jessa, flashed Liam a sympathetic smile through the passenger window. She opened the passenger door and clambered out, her round belly preceding her.

"Jessa! It's too cold! Stay inside," Lincoln called, but Jessa ignored him.

Before Liam could pull away, she'd wrapped him in a bear hug, or as close to a bear hug as she could manage. He inhaled the familiar scent of her signature perfume—a sweet floral scent she'd told him once was jasmine.

He didn't want to admit how long it had been since another human had touched him. Stiff and awkward, he patted her back.

"I'm so happy you came, Liam." She pulled away, gripped his shoulders, and looked up into his face. "It's been far too long since we've seen you."

Even nine months pregnant, Jessa Coleman was the most beautiful woman he'd ever known. Her long black braids hung down her back and framed her face, her pink coat bringing out the warm brown of her skin. Her features were friendly and open, her smile always bright.

Not for the first time, he wondered what a woman like this was doing anywhere near him and his brother. Another stab of regret struck him. All these years, and he'd never met anyone else like her. He would never begrudge his brother an iota of happiness, but his own loneliness had never stung quite so intensely.

She reached down for his suitcase. "Here let me help you."

He grasped the handle first. "I don't need—"

"I'll help." She flashed him a sharp look and followed him to the trunk of the car. She leaned into the trunk, moving aside Lincoln's gym bag and a few odds and ends.

Liam set his suitcase inside the trunk and unzipped it. From a netted inner pocket, he tugged out the small everyday carry case that contained his multitool, stainless steel tactical pen, small LED flashlight, two lighters, small folding knife, and a handkerchief wound with paracord. He tucked it into his coat pocket.

3

He wanted to take his Glock 19 out of its case and holster it to his hip, but with Chicago's strict gun laws, he couldn't. He was tempted to concealed-carry anyway, but a cop directing traffic not thirty feet to his right dissuaded him.

"How is he?" Liam asked quietly.

A shadow passed across Jessa's face. "Getting worse."

Liam tensed. This was the news he'd dreaded. While with the 101st, Lincoln did two tours in Afghanistan, while Liam served as a Delta Special Forces Operator. After eight years of seeing too much and doing worse, Liam was medically discharged for a back injury. Five crushed discs from jumping from choppers and airplanes with Special Forces. He was still strong enough to lift a house, but he'd slowed a step or two.

Neither man came back the same. Lincoln, though, had returned home in worse shape. While Liam knew he was scarred, Lincoln insisted on acting like he was fine—he always had, even when they were kids, and the secrets they kept made them anything but fine.

Lincoln's carefully cultivated optimism masked far deeper problems. Six years ago, he'd returned home with a prosthetic limb after an IED explosion took out his best friend and the lower half of his right leg. The PTSD that followed was the gift that kept on giving.

Jessa touched his arm. "He needs you here."

When Jessa had called him yesterday, she'd sounded worried. She was the steadiest person he knew. She was calm and capable, and one of the best obstetricians at Northwestern Medicine Prentice Women's Hospital.

If she was this concerned, the problem with Lincoln was serious. Liam had known he had to come, no matter what.

He far preferred to drive anywhere he needed to go, but his

junky 2001 Chevrolet Silverado had engine trouble he hadn't managed to fix yet. With his truck undependable for any distance over twenty miles, he'd dropped everything and taken the next available flight from Cherry Capital Airport in Traverse City to O'Hare.

A single glance at his brother through the car window, and he knew. Identical twins, they shared the exact same rugged handsomeness. The broad shoulders and lean, wiry strength they'd inherited from their father; the angular bone structure, piercing gray-blue eyes, and thick chestnut hair from their mother.

Lincoln looked like he'd lost fifteen pounds since the last time Liam had seen him. His cheekbones were too sharp. The shadows rimming his bloodshot eyes and the wan pallor of his skin weren't from genetics.

"He's been having nightmares—violent ones," Jessa said. "He barely sleeps. He had an outburst at work. They laid him off. He doesn't want you to know."

Lincoln worked as a security consultant for a couple of Fortune 500 companies located on the Loop, the business district of Chicago. Liam could never keep straight which ones.

"He still won't go to the support group or see the therapist Veterans Affairs provided. And with the baby coming..." her voice trailed off, her face tense.

Guilt speared him. After four years apart, Liam was finally less than ten feet from his brother. He'd never felt the distance so completely. While he'd been nursing his own private wounds, his brother had been floundering. Liam hadn't known how bad it was. That was on him.

"If you could talk to him? Please. You're the only one who can."

A car honked behind them.

"I'll try. I promise." He zipped the suitcase and closed the trunk but kept his backpack with him. It was his go-bag and contained his emergency essentials. He never traveled without it.

Liam shoved his hands in his pockets. His fingers brushed something soft. "Hey. Before I forget." He pulled the soft object out and stuffed it awkwardly into her hands. "Didn't have time to wrap it."

He liked making things with his hands. Mostly, woodworking and construction projects. He'd built his own kitchen table and chairs. He'd learned to make his own soap and shampoo, too. This winter, he'd turned to knitting blankets.

She unfolded the knit cap he'd been working on ever since Lincoln had texted that 'they' were pregnant that summer. It was lopsided, with a few bulgy, crooked spots, but the tiny blue and green striped hat was at least recognizable as a hat.

"Should've practiced more. Was planning on it, but—"

"He's gonna love it, Liam. I love it." A radiant smile spread across her face. It warmed him from the inside out. He smelled her perfume again—that familiar whiff of jasmine that made his heart ache.

They hurried into the car to avoid more irritated honking. Liam slipped off his backpack and set it on the seat beside him. Lincoln twisted around and offered his hand in greeting. "Long time no see, brother."

It was formal and stiff and far too insignificant compared to what lay between them. Emotions rose in Liam's chest—remorse, guilt, fierce love. He longed to lean forward and grab his twin in a powerful embrace, to tell him how sorry he was, that he was here for him now, no matter what.

He did none of those things. From stubborn hardheadedness

or embarrassment or shame, he didn't know. Instead, he took Lincoln's proffered hand and shook it. "Good to see you again."

A few minutes later, they were driving along I-90 toward downtown. Traffic crowded the lanes on either side of them. Liam watched the hunched buildings, the train tracks easing by on his left, the people waiting at the stations buried in heavy coats, scarves, gloves, and hats.

He didn't like crowds, and he didn't like cities—they made him nervous, reminded him of the stress and urgency of his time overseas, where you were never safe and anyone might be your enemy—man, woman, or child.

His restless fingers drumming the steering wheel, Lincoln kept up a stream of innocuous questions about Liam's flight, the inadequacy of the in-flight snacks, and the length of the security lines, but his bloodshot eyes kept flicking toward Liam in the backseat.

That was Lincoln—filling up the uncomfortable spaces with inconsequential babble, pretending everything was okay, even if the roof was caving in on them.

He'd been that way since they were kids, when they both wished they could pretend the fighting and screaming outside their bedroom door didn't exist.

They turned onto West Jackson Blvd. The Sears Tower appeared several blocks ahead of them, the black aluminum and bronze-tinted glass skyscraper soaring one hundred and ten stories above them. Supposedly it was the Willis Tower now, but he didn't care.

"Weather's getting pretty bad." Lincoln leaned forward and peered at the thickening clouds, the layer of fog wrapping the tops of the skyscrapers like tulle. "Good thing your flight wasn't delayed."

"There's another big snowstorm coming in," Jessa said. "It's going to be freezing cold for weeks with temps well below zero. Record breaking cold. It's crazy."

Liam stared at the brick apartment buildings crawling by outside the window, the harsh sounds of honking horns and jabbering jackhammers assaulting his ears. The ornate white stone of Union Station slid by, the sidewalks crowded with tourists and holiday shoppers.

He wished he had something to say. He wished he could take back the last four years, wished he could fix whatever had gone so wrong between them.

"You hungry, Liam?" Lincoln asked. "We're headed for Giordano's for an early lunch. You can't visit Chi-Town without some deep-dish pizza. We thought we'd stroll along the magnificent mile and visit Millennium Park and the Bean before dinner. We have reservations at The Metropolitan Club at five with Jessa's parents. You remember them from the wedding?"

Liam shifted uncomfortably in his seat. He was tired from the strain of traveling, the drain of being surrounded by so many people, so many potential threats. He was angry with himself and worried sick about Lincoln. Sightseeing was the last thing on his mind.

"You don't have to go through all this for me. I don't need—"

"Nonsense!" Lincoln boomed too loudly. "You're in a beautiful city on Christmas Eve! You think we'd let you bum around in our boring, cramped apartment?"

That was exactly what Liam wanted, but he didn't say so. He told himself that he was here for Lincoln. And for Jessa. Whatever Lincoln needed of him, he would do. He would simply have to endure the next several hours of forced socializing. He'd done it plenty of times before.

"We were going to take you to the Skydeck. Pretty sure you won't see four different states in this weather. We'll try again tomorrow—if the baby hasn't made his appearance, anyway."

"This baby have a name?" Liam asked, grasping for some common ground.

Jessa turned to look at him and rolled her eyes. "You know your brother can't decide on anything."

"I'll know when I see him." Lincoln babbled on about various tourist attractions and sights, his rising voice filling the car. Liam's gut twisted. He saw right through his brother's façade. The more anxious or upset Lincoln got, the louder and faster he talked.

Even though they were twins, beyond their identical physical appearance, they were nothing alike. Lincoln had always been the friendly, social, outgoing one. Liam was the opposite. He was still and quiet, serious and thoughtful.

Fresh regret churned in his gut. He was a terrible brother. He'd failed Lincoln. He shouldn't have stayed away so long.

He wasn't good with people. Never had been. But that was just an excuse.

After their parents died seven years ago, the two people sitting in this car were the last two people he loved in the world. He'd spent so much time avoiding things he didn't want to face that he'd missed out on what really mattered.

He would do better now. He wouldn't let his own stubbornness get in the way again. He'd talk to Lincoln and fix this—

"What the heck?" Lincoln said. "What's up with the dashboard?"

Liam glanced toward the front of the car. The digital screen behind the steering wheel blinked off, then on, then stayed off.

The car jolted with a grinding sound Liam had never heard before.

"Hey!" Jessa yelped. "What's going on?"

"Something's wrong!" Lincoln wrenched the steering wheel. "The dashboard isn't working! The wheel is stuck—"

Something huge smashed into the back of their car.

2

A terrible wrenching sound filled the car. Metal scraped against metal. Jessa screamed.

The Audi surged forward, punched by whatever car or truck had rammed into it from behind.

"I can't stop!" Lincoln slammed his foot against the brakes. Nothing happened. "Nothing works!"

The Audi bore down on the white SUV directly ahead of them. Liam had only an instant to brace himself against the side and the back of the front seat before impact.

They crashed into the SUV. His head struck the back of the seat. Whiplash burned his neck.

He blinked hard, raised his head. Pain radiated down his spine. He groaned, instinctively feeling his ribs and his skull, searching for fractures or open wounds. Nothing.

Things came back into focus slowly. The tan leather seats. His go-bag flung to the floor. Gray daylight streaming through the rear windows.

The windshield was cracked. Steam poured from the smashed

hood. He could just make out the crumpled rear of the white SUV through the billowing cloud of steam. Twisting around in his seat, he saw the vehicle that had struck them—a huge black Chevy Suburban had crushed their trunk. The Audi was likely totaled.

Liam forced himself to focus on Lincoln and Jessa. Their airbags hadn't deployed. Either the vehicle hadn't been going fast enough, or something had malfunctioned.

He leaned forward. "Lincoln? Jessa?"

Lincoln responded with a groan of his own. He raised his head and looked around. "Jessa? Jessa, you okay?"

She didn't answer.

Lincoln leaned over the console, touched her shoulder. A small cut sliced across his forehead, blood dripping down the side of his temple. His face was tight with panic. "Babe?"

Jessa moved. She coughed and lifted her head. Her hands flew to her belly. She prodded her stomach, then sank back against the seat in relief.

A long red line streaked her neck from the seat belt, but she didn't seem to feel it. Her only concern was the baby.

"He's okay," she whispered. "I just felt him."

"And you?" Liam asked.

"Yeah...just...shaken up. I don't...what happened?"

Outside the windows, none of the other vehicles were moving. The traffic light on the pole ahead had gone dark.

"I don't know! Everything just—stopped." Lincoln pounded the steering wheel angrily. "It's only three years old. I don't get it. How could the dashboard screen, the brakes, and the power steering all fail at once?"

"We should get out," Liam said slowly. He lifted his go-bag off the floor and plunked it on the seat beside him. It felt like he was moving through molasses. "Something's wrong."

"I just crashed the car with my pregnant wife inside it!" Lincoln spat. "I know something's wrong, damn it! It's the stupid car."

Liam shoved open the rear passenger door, unbuckled his seat belt, and eased gingerly to his feet. The freezing cold bit at him. Aches and pains made themselves known across his back and shoulders. He felt like some giant hand had tossed him across the room.

Sounds of screaming and shouting echoed in the crisp air. Dozens of cars had crashed. Those that hadn't were trapped between the various pileups of five, seven, and ten or more cars. Drivers were either still in their cars, shell-shocked or injured, or standing next to their vehicles, shouting at the other drivers.

On the sidewalks, pedestrians had stopped walking. They stood in groups and clusters, mouths gaping, staring and pointing at the various accidents. Some had their phones out and were waving them around or shaking them. A few looked like they were trying to call 911.

Liam scanned both sides of the road. Tall buildings towered above them, crowded in on both sides. He felt closed in, cut off.

Anxiety twisted in his gut. "Doesn't look like the buildings on either side of the street have power. No lights."

"Local power outage. Must be." Lincoln climbed out of the car and turned in a slow circle, his eyes widening as he took in the carnage.

"Not to cars."

"It's because the traffic lights went out."

The intersection of Jackson and Wacker behind them was packed with crashed vehicles. Ahead of them, several cars had drifted onto the sidewalk in order to avoid hitting the vehicle ahead of them, narrowly missing pedestrians.

Traffic was at a standstill. No one was moving.

"Traffic lights wouldn't cause all this," Liam said.

"I see working cars." Lincoln's voice was high and tight, like he was desperately trying to convince himself more than anyone else. He was jumpy, his eyes darting from one thing to the next. "Look at that guy in his classic pimped out Pontiac Firebird Trans Am screaming at everyone else to move out of his way. As if they can with all the other cars blocking the road."

The Firebird's engine was still running, but the wreck of cars ahead and behind prevented him from moving. A few other older model cars appeared to be working. They might as well have stalled too, for all the good it would do them.

A group of Asian tourists bundled in brightly colored hats and scarves on the corner were lifting their phones toward the sky, like that would help them get a better signal. Others frowned at their phones, tapping the screens in confusion.

"I can't get through!" a woman on the opposite side of the street shouted. She dropped her armload of shopping bags and jabbed at her phone. "Someone needs to call 911!"

"I can't get through either," said a middle-aged man in a tweed coat standing beside his stalled Mercedes. A C-shaped cut marred his clean-shaven cheek. He shook his phone like that would help. "My phone won't even power up. The system's overloaded or something. Maybe this power outage happened all over the city."

A Hispanic woman in her sixties wearing a shiny purple coat stumbled out of the white SUV they'd hit. She braced both hands against the hood, leaned forward, and vomited.

"I need to see if she's okay," Jessa said as she opened the front passenger door. She was in doctor mode, already scanning the street to see who else needed medical attention.

A mother and father hunched over a young boy slumped

on the curb, blood coursing down the side of his head. A hipster sat in the middle of the road amid shattered glass, groaning and clutching a leg bent at an unnatural, horrible angle.

"You need to take care of yourself," Lincoln said. "Stay inside the car until we figure out what to do. It's warmer. You have to think of the baby."

She ignored him and pulled at her seatbelt. "I can't get out. My seatbelt is locked or something...I'm stuck."

"Just a sec, honey." Lincoln didn't move. He took out his phone, his hands shaking. "I'll call for an ambulance."

"Good idea," Jessa said calmly. "There could be internal injuries or concussions. Just because we feel okay doesn't mean we are."

"Where's the nearest hospital? There's no way an ambulance is getting through the streets like this."

"Mercy is a few miles south of us on Michigan Ave," Jessa said. "Rush is a few miles west. Northwestern is directly north off Michigan Avenue two miles, maybe a bit more. I want Northwestern. Take me to Prentice on East Superior. I'll get the best care there."

"We may need to walk," Liam said.

"I can walk," Jessa said. "I just have to get out of this damn car."

He pulled out his own phone. The screen was frozen, filled with weird zigzagging lines and squiggles in strange colors.

Lincoln glared down at his phone. "Damn it! Nothing's working. Must be the blackout is affecting the towers."

"It's not the towers. Or it's not only the towers. It's bigger than that."

Liam cocked his head and listened. No horns. No rumbling

machinery. No growl of engines. The racket of confused and fearful voices were the only sounds.

The mechanical din of the city had gone silent.

The dull sense of dread swirling in his stomach grew stronger. This wasn't an isolated event. It sounded like the entire city had gone dark all at once. But it wasn't just the electricity. If cars and phones were affected, too...

"An EMP," he said slowly.

"A what?" Jessa asked as she struggled with her seat belt.

"An electromagnetic pulse. From a high-altitude nuclear explosion or a coronal mass ejection from the sun. Must be an EMP though, not a CME. Cars would probably still be working if it was a solar flare. And phones."

"No way." Lincoln shook his head fiercely, his mouth pressed into a thin line. He glared daggers at Liam. "This isn't one of your paranoid fantasies. This is real life! Get a grip!"

"Look around you!" Liam snapped.

He'd always believed in being prepared. Growing up in a chaotic household meant he'd learned early that no one was coming to save him—not even his own parents. He needed to be able to save himself.

If his obsessive research had taught him one thing, it was that people liked to think they were right, but people didn't know what they didn't know. Some people thought an EMP would destroy every electronic device in the country, no matter how small. Other people believed an EMP would only take out the electrical grid, and maybe only regionally.

In reality, not even nuclear physicists and scientific experts knew what would happen for sure.

"We just need to be calm and figure this out." But Lincoln's words belied his actions. He was shaking, his hands clenching and unclenching his fists at his sides. His eyes bulged. "Everything will be fine. This is just a local power outage and some fender-benders. It's under control. Everything's under control."

But nothing was under control. All he needed to do was look around to see that. And things would only get worse.

Liam had felt uncomfortable without his pistol before. Now everything had changed. He needed to be prepared for anything. He strode around to the rear of their vehicle, the rear end smashed and crumpled.

There was no getting into the trunk by popping it open the usual way. The electronic key likely wouldn't work, anyway. Not much else was working.

A spiderweb of cracks crisscrossed the rear window. He took his tactical pen/glass breaker out of his everyday carry case, wedged himself between the crashed Suburban and their vehicle to get as close to the trunk as he could with the big grille of the Suburban still smashed into the left side of the Audi, and used it to punch through the weakened glass.

Gummy shards rained into the trunk compartment as the rest of the rear windshield collapsed. With his gloved hands, he brushed enough glass out of the way on the right side to reach in and unlock his suitcase. He dropped the steel pen into his pocket and fumbled for the gun case.

He pulled out the gun and holster and left the case. He had extra magazines in his go-bag. He grabbed his tactical knife and sheath and attached them to his belt, where they belonged.

Someone screamed—a loud, piercing shriek that cut through the confused din like a knife through butter.

Liam whirled toward the sound, his heart jolting in his chest.

A teenage boy with a mohawk and rings in his ears pointed above Liam's head at something behind him, something in the sky.

3

L iam spun around, yanked himself free of the rear window, and shielded his eyes with his free hand. Shards of glass stuck to his coat and gloves. He didn't bother to brush them off.

The fog swirled like a gray haze, blurring the sky visible between the tall buildings into an indistinct haze. The clouds above them were thick, heavy, and dark, signaling another looming snowstorm.

But it wasn't the clouds that captured his attention.

Looking west along Jackson Blvd, Sears Tower loomed ahead, and to the left, another huge but less familiar skyscraper. The river was just beyond, out of sight. Several shorter office and residential buildings blocked the horizon line.

In the wide square of sky, a plane soared silently overhead, the nose angled downward. It was hard to tell how far away it was, but it couldn't have been more than a half-mile. Maybe less.

It was flying close and low—so low, it looked like it was barely skimming the tops of the skyscrapers.

People screamed and ducked. There was no time to react or

respond in any other way. Liam crouched behind the rear of the car, gun in hand, adrenaline shooting through his system.

The plane nose-dived. With a crack like thunder, the huge aircraft smashed into Union Station. The cacophonous *boom* shattered the air.

The explosion engulfed the aircraft in a flaming ball of fire that swelled into the street. Debris and ash mushroomed. Black smoke billowed above the buildings and poured into the sky.

"What was that?" someone cried.

"What's going on?" a woman shouted.

"A plane just crashed," said a man several feet to Liam's left. His Honda Pilot had bumped into the blue Altima ahead of him, barely denting the bumper. His car was just as stalled as all the others. "Holy hell. This thing must be affecting everything with electronics."

Liam straightened. "That's my guess."

"Did all the planes stop working, too?" Jessa asked from inside the car. She'd left the door open despite Lincoln's instructions.

"Must be," the guy said, his voice trembling, his expression stricken. "Their electronic systems must be fried—altimeters, communications, their instrument displays gone completely dark. Damn. That plane must have lost all power and gone into a stall."

The man ran a shaky hand through his thinning hair. He was a black guy in his mid-fifties, wearing a puffy orange coat, jeans, and a Chicago Bears scarf wound around his neck. "There are back-up systems. Depending on the plane, they should have the ability to lower a ram-air turbine to give them limited system power. But if their screen processors are fried, they'd have to use their stand-by instruments, but with newer planes, even those are connected to glass screens—new tech—so they'd be fried, too."

He turned to Liam with a heavy sigh. "Name's David Jenkins. I'm a pilot for Delta. It's my day off."

"Nice to meet you," Jessa said politely. "It looked like it was flying right over our heads."

"Perception and angle account for what people think they're seeing. Happens all the time." David adjusted his glasses and rubbed his hands together like he could stop their trembling. "That was too close for comfort. There are probably dozens—hundreds—of planes in holding patterns right now, desperate to land."

"Are more planes going to start falling from the sky, then?" Jessa asked, fear in her voice. "Aren't there around five thousand planes in the air over the United States alone at any given time?"

"Could be," David said. "Newer planes are 'fly by wire' systems, with most of the control of the aircraft done by computer. Some of the older models will be able to maintain some functions. They won't just tailspin and pancake into the ground. All aircraft should be controllable with complete electrical failure. Doesn't mean everything works like it's supposed to when the crap hits the fan, though.

"They're made to be stable, so they can glide down—or at least try. Most pilots will go for a remote airfield or try a military one away from major cities if they can. If they've got somewhere to land and clear line of sight, some of 'em will get down safely."

"But not all of them," Jessa said.

The man's gaze flicked to the smoke-filled sky. "Clearly."

Liam had read conflicting information about planes. Much of it depended on the strength of the EMP, which was still a very large unknown. Military aircraft were hardened against an EMP attack, but civilian aircraft weren't.

20

Truth was, no one knew what would happen with absolute certainty.

"Where's Lincoln?" Jessa asked. "He was just right here."

If they were walking to the nearest hospital, they needed protection. Liam turned back to the trunk, reached through the shattered window and dug through his carefully organized suitcase. He slipped three more preloaded magazines into his coat pockets.

He jacked a magazine into his Glock, chambered a round, took out the magazine and thumbed in another round. One in the chamber, seventeen in the magazine. Eighteen shots.

David watched him curiously but said nothing. He wasn't stupid. He knew everything had changed in a heartbeat. But like everyone else, he wasn't yet sure how.

Liam holstered his pistol and tucked his coat over it. It was concealed but close at hand if need be. He knew enough about human nature to realize it wouldn't be long until panic set in.

He, Lincoln, and Jessa needed to be long gone by then.

"Lincoln!" he said. "Time to go."

Lincoln didn't answer.

"There's another one!" a tourist shouted from the sidewalk.

Several people gasped and pointed. Liam whirled around.

A second plane emerged through the thick clouds to the west. It hung suspended in the sky, so close Liam imagined he could see the panicked passengers staring out the windows.

"Damn it!" Liam's heartbeat quickened. "It looks huge."

David craned his neck to look up. "These big aircraft are sixty feet tall, with wingspans of two hundred feet and just as long. Top speed up to five hundred and twelve knots—that's close to six hundred miles per hour, though it's probably only going four hundred now. We're still talking a payload close to six hundred thousand pounds."

"Looks like it's headed straight for us. That another perception warp?"

David shook his head, his mouth twisting, eyes going big and round behind his glasses. He took a step backward, then another. He bumped into the Altima. "That isn't a perception warp."

Liam went still. "What?"

"He must be trying to land in Lake Michigan," David said, his voice rising in barely restrained panic. "But he's not gonna make it. Holy hell. He's aiming right for us!"

Fear constricted Liam's lungs, his heart tightening like a fist. David was right. The pilot might've been fighting to lift the nose from its downward glide, but it wasn't working.

The plane floated closer, eerily silent. The nose dipped lower and lower.

The plane was going down.

And it was going down right on top of them.

"Run!" David shouted. He turned to the stunned crowd and flailed his arms. "Run! Go! Go!"

Panicked screams filled the air as hundreds of people turned and fled. Cell phones and shopping bags fell to the ground, utterly forgotten.

Mothers seized their sons' and daughters' hands. Fathers grabbed their toddlers and preschoolers as they ran. Men and women pushed each other to get through the slog of vehicles and packed sidewalks.

An elderly woman fell. A man stooped to help her to her feet, pushing back the crowd. Packs of people swirled around them and kept going.

"I'm still stuck!" Jessa cried.

Terror and dread thrummed through Liam's veins. He didn't freeze or flee—he switched into soldier mode, his years of training coming back like muscle memory. Don't panic. Assess the situation. Get your people and get the hell out.

He whipped around, searching for Lincoln. Where the hell was he? He wasn't on the sidewalks, wasn't one of the people struggling out of their cars or racing down the middle of the avenue.

David's wild gaze darted from Jessa trapped in the car to Liam. He backed away, hands up in a gesture of surrender—or helplessness. "I'm sorry, man! I'm sorry!"

David spun and fled with the crowds, a bright orange blotch among hundreds.

Liam couldn't run. Not without Jessa. Not without his brother.

Think, damn it, think! Lincoln had been standing on the other side of their Audi just a minute ago—

Adrenaline pouring through his veins, Liam dashed around the car, slip-sliding on the icy road. He rounded the bumper to find his brother flat on the ground, curled into a fetal position, hands over his head. His eyes were opened but wide and glassy, and staring at nothing.

He crouched beside his brother and shook his shoulders. Nothing.

"Lincoln!" he shouted.

He slapped him hard in the face. No response.

His brother was stuck in that trauma-induced fugue he knew well from childhood. When it got so bad that he couldn't deal, his brother just went away somewhere inside his head.

The first plane's explosion must've triggered it. The PTSD had only made it worse.

Panic threatened to overtake him. It would take minutes—maybe longer—to pull Lincoln out of it. Until then, he was no better than a dead weight.

Liam would have to drag him out of the line of fire.

The reality of his situation struck him like a gut-punch. Jessa was nine months pregnant. She could barely walk, let alone run. She was still trapped in the car.

She needed his help. So did Lincoln.

He couldn't save them both.

Blood rushed in his ears. His pounding heart felt like it was about to hammer right out of his chest. Fear and indecision warred within him, freezing him in place.

The plane plummeted, silent death about to descend upon their heads.

A hundred memories of combat flashed through his head simultaneously—fiery explosions, billowing smoke, bullets zinging past his skull, the agonized screams of his brothers in arms, every second a life-or-death decision, every move possibly the last one you'd ever make.

It was a split-second decision. One that would haunt him for the rest of his life. If he didn't make this choice, Lincoln would hate him forever.

Either way, Liam already hated himself.

He leapt to his feet and sprinted around to the other side of the car. He left his brother behind.

4

L iam already had his tactical knife out as he crouched beside the opened passenger door.

"Where's Lincoln?" Jessa cried. "Where is he?"

Liam sawed through the seatbelt strap below her swollen belly, hating himself for not freeing her long before. It was a mistake. And it would cost them.

The belt released. He grabbed her hands and jerked her from the car. "Run! Go!"

She twisted back, aghast. "Lincoln!"

No time to explain or waste precious energy. If they didn't go now, they were both dead.

Liam wrapped his arm around her ribs beneath her arms and dragged her, half-running, half-stumbling. They fled down the street, zigzagging around the crashed vehicles to the sidewalk. He took in their surroundings in a frantic heartbeat, analyzing the options for flaws and strengths.

The next block was still hundreds of yards east. The office and residential buildings looming on either side of them were twelve to fifteen stories tall and crowded in close like the walls of a giant maze herding them in a single direction.

The only way was forward, toward Michigan Avenue and the shoreline. They'd have to take shelter in one of the storefronts lining the road and hope for the best.

He had no clue which building would provide the best cover, didn't know exactly where the monstrous plane would land or how. He was acutely aware that rather than leading them away from it, he could be leading them directly into the oncoming path of destruction instead.

Giordano's was on the right with its red awning on the first floor of a twelve-story masonry office building. A narrow alley lay just beyond it, but a trolley had crashed into the corner of the next building, completely blocking access.

The cold air burned his throat with every ragged gasp. The smells of the street filled his nostrils—pizza and breadsticks, fresh donuts and coffee—all of it bizarre and disconcerting in the face of such destruction and chaos.

He glimpsed David's bright orange coat ducking into the glass-fronted restaurant. Too much shrapnel. Not enough brick and stone for protection.

There. Just past the shiny glass restaurant façade—a tall building of reddish stone. Maybe a bank or office suites.

It didn't matter what it was. They were running out of options.

Liam swerved sharply right, dragging Jessa with him. He jerked open the glass door with one hand, already pushing her through ahead of him.

Off-balance and awkward, she stumbled and nearly fell. He still had her arm and hauled her up and forward.

The inside looked like the lobby of an office building—fancy pillars and marble floors and huge potted plants. He spotted a heavy granite counter at the far end.

A couple of office workers in tailored suits gaped at the windows beside a row of potted plants wound with Christmas lights. A handful of fleeing pedestrians had entered ahead of them and paused inside the entrance, unsure what to do next or where to go.

One of the office workers took several hesitant steps back from the window, her hand over her throat, eyes wide and stunned.

He pushed Jessa inside. "Get to the back!"

Jessa ran as best she could, lumbering, breathing heavily, arms wind-milling like she could grasp the air and make herself go faster.

"The plane's about to crash!" someone shouted.

He should've kept running. But some darkly fascinated part of him froze on the sidewalk, half-inside, the door half-open, his heart jackhammering against his ribcage.

He looked back.

The plane careened toward them, the nose tilted down. The wide white belly skimmed the roof of a fourteen-story building a few blocks behind them.

Everything faded away, funneling into a single moment—the plane, huge and terrible and utterly silent, plunging like a hawk toward its prey.

And then it hit.

The left wing struck the side of the Sears Tower at several hundred miles per hour. The lightweight aluminum wing sheared completely off, snapping like a child's toy.

The plane twisted and wrenched as it plummeted. A horrible grinding, shrieking sound filled the air like a great dragon screaming overhead.

Several thousand pounds of screeching metal ripped into the buildings, metal crumbling and tearing. Huge chunks of aluminum and glass spewed into the air.

The right wing tore from the fuselage. It spun end over end, mowing down a dozen fleeing people like ants before smashing into a glass store front.

The body of the plane smashed between the narrow buildings and ploughed into the ground. A great red cloud like molten lava exploded several stories into the air.

Fiery hunks of the plane hurtled in every direction like cannon balls, punching through glass storefronts, pelting the street, crushing cars, striking fleeing pedestrians and trapping them beneath chunks of smoldering metal.

Pure, unadulterated terror pierced Liam straight through the heart.

He spun and sprinted inside.

He wouldn't make it. The roaring cacophony of death was right on his heels.

A horrendous, ear-splitting roar engulfed everything. The floor vibrated beneath his feet. Windows shattered. Massive chunks of shrapnel as large as cars pummeled the exterior walls, crumbling mortar and stone.

He dove behind a marble pillar ten yards inside and flattened himself belly-first against the floor, hands over his head and face, fingers laced behind his neck.

Nothing but dumb luck would save him now.

5

L iam rose unsteadily to his feet, stunned and dazed, his ears ringing.

His back ached from the car accident and the jarring fall to the marble floor. A half-dozen cuts marred his hands and forearms. He plucked a thumb-sized shard of glass from his right thigh just above the knee.

He didn't even feel the sting. The injuries were all superficial. Most of the shrapnel had blasted over his prone form.

He was alive. He was fine.

People were speaking, yelling and shouting and crying, but he barely heard them. Everything sounded tinny and far away. Smoke drifted everywhere, clogging his throat. He pressed his arm over his face and mouth and coughed violently.

He didn't know how much time had passed—seconds or minutes or even longer.

"Jessa!" he grunted. Then louder. "Jessa!"

Several large pieces of debris had peeled off and rocketed

through the lobby's front windows with tremendous force. A huge hunk of engine fan blade had jettisoned into one of the corner offices, imploding the glass walls and demolishing the wooden desk.

Two people had hidden behind it. One was crushed to death. The other leaned against the wall, cradling a broken arm, his face a mangled mess of broken bone and bloodied flesh.

Several other survivors had sustained serious cuts, scrapes, and puncture wounds from flying glass and shredded bits of metal and plastic. He smelled blood and dust and things burning.

Apprehension gripped him. He didn't see his sister-in-law.

"JESSA!"

"I'm...here."

He maneuvered through the debris to the rear of the lobby in front of a bank of elevators. He crouched beside her and quickly assessed her condition.

She lay on the marble floor on her back, breathing heavily and holding her distended belly. Dust and a bit of blood smeared her face. Small cuts peppered her cheeks and neck.

A bloodstain the size of his fist stained her coat over her right shoulder. More quarter-sized droplets spattered her right arm and torso.

She was clearly injured, but he didn't see anything fatal.

"You were supposed to hide behind the granite counter!"

"I fell. I couldn't make it in time."

He shook his head. His anger was at himself. He'd stopped to look. She'd gone on alone. "Let's go."

"I don't hear sirens," she said. "Where are the ambulances and firetrucks?"

"They don't work because of the EMP. First responders will come, but they'll be on foot. It'll take longer." He rose to his feet and held out his hand to help her up. "You said the hospital is two miles away. That's where we need to go."

"Liam."

He looked down at her.

She met his gaze, a resigned bleakness in her eyes that terrified him.

"What is it?"

She moved the right flap of her long coat aside. A twisted piece of metal the size of his hand jutted from her inner left thigh, halfway between her knee and crotch. Bright red blood swelled across her leg, pulsing with her heartbeat.

Her huge coat had hidden the large puddle spreading beneath her. But he saw it now. He saw it all with a horrible clarity.

His whole body went cold. Dread slicked his insides. He stared at her in alarm. "Jessa."

Jessa shifted her leg with a grimace. Fresh blood poured from the gash and splashed onto the floor. "It lacerated my femoral artery."

He cursed softly. "Don't move."

He had hemostatic gauze and Celox granules for blood-clotting in his pack, but it wouldn't be enough. Not the way the blood pulsed from the wound, gushing like a hose.

"Okay." She grimaced, teeth gritted, and nodded to herself as if coming to terms with the gravity of her situation. "Okay. Don't remove the shrapnel yet. It's likely burning hot and could be pressing against the artery, preventing further bleeding."

"You need a tourniquet."

"We have to get to the hospital within ninety minutes. Prolonged ischemia of the tissue at and below the tourniquet may lead to permanent muscle damage and necrosis."

"We will." He removed his gloves, shucked the backpack from

his shoulders, and unzipped it. He dug through his emergency supplies for the medical kit as quickly as he could, his fingers numb from shock and terror. He opened the red zippered pouch, removed a CAT tourniquet from his bag, and ripped open the packaging.

She seized his arm with surprising strength. "Where's Lincoln? Where's my husband?"

"He's on his way," Liam lied. It just about killed him to lie to her, but he saw no other choice. "He made it to the Dunkin' Donuts. He'll be here any minute."

She needed to focus on her own survival—and the baby's. Worry would only make things worse. So would the truth.

Liam shoved that thought down deep. He couldn't think of Lincoln now. He couldn't afford to lose his focus, not with Jessa depending on him.

Moving swiftly, he placed the tourniquet three inches above the wound, pulled the initial strap through the buckle as tight as possible, and tightened, turning the windlass several times, increasing the pressure until finally the arterial blood flow slowed.

"Now, the shrapnel," Jessa said through clenched teeth. "Leaving it in will cause more damage every time I move."

He nodded stiffly. He knew what to do.

He gathered the clotting gauze and a bandage wrap from his go-bag and made sure they were ready to use. He yanked off his scarf and wound it around his hand to shield his skin from the hot, razor-sharp metal.

Jessa didn't close her eyes or turn away as he pulled the shrapnel from her thigh. She sucked in a sharp, pained breath.

He hated causing her pain, but there was nothing to be done except to move quickly and efficiently. Applying pressure as best he could, he checked the blood flow. It was still bleeding too much. He tightened the tourniquet, then packed the jagged wound with the gauze and wrapped her leg.

"Where is he?" she said again when he'd finished. "Why isn't he here?"

He wasn't any good at pep talks. He wiped his hands clean with a disinfectant wipe, carefully replaced the medical kit but kept it on top of the other supplies—she might need it again—and hoisted his backpack.

He tugged on his gloves, rose to his feet, and held out his hand.

She refused to take it. She pressed her lips together and frowned up at him. "Liam—"

"He'll meet us at the hospital," he said with as much conviction as possible, like if they both believed it, it would be true. "We just need to get there."

She nodded, her chin jutting with that stubborn determination that had always driven Lincoln nuts, but had never bothered Liam. In the sandbox of Afghanistan, a stubborn refusal to quit had kept him alive more times than he could count. Hopefully it would keep her alive, too.

She grasped his hand, and he hauled her up. She took an unsteady step. Her brown skin was ashen, her eyes too wide, her pupils huge.

The floor beneath her was smeared and splattered with blood. Blood soaked her leg and her coat. Too much blood. It was everywhere. More blood outside of a human body than should be possible.

He'd seen that much blood in warzones overseas. Too many times. And every time, they'd lost the gravely injured operator. Not Jessa. It wouldn't happen to Jessa. He wouldn't allow it.

Fear clawed at his throat, choking off his breath. He pushed down the rising panic. He had to act, had to save her. No way was he letting her die. Not after Lincoln.

He would get her to the hospital. No other choice.

It was her only chance.

6

They stepped outside the office building into hell. Wisps of gray fog unfurled above the looming skyscrapers on either side, trapping them in an eerie apocalyptic nightmare.

The bitter cold blasted Liam's exposed face and neck. He nearly choked on the acrid fumes of thousands of gallons of burnt aviation gas. It burned his nostrils and seared his throat.

The keening wails and moans of the wounded and dying shattered the cold stillness left in the void of no car engines, no honking horns, no dull rumble of construction.

Death was everywhere. The horrific images seared his eyes, his brain.

He forced himself to look west toward the Audi, toward where he'd left his twin behind.

The street was unrecognizable. Where once was a road, cars, sidewalks, streetlights, and bustling pedestrians was now a blackened, scorched, and gaping maw. Deep gouges marred the buildings on either side of Jackson Blvd, like the stone, steel, and glass had been carved apart by a giant's blade.

The leaked jet fuel had ignited in a massive fireball. Flames licked the sky as black oily smoke poured from the mechanical monster's guts. The remains of the plane rose above him in a mountain of rent metal and twisted, melted fiberglass.

Dozens of vehicles were obliterated beneath the crash site. There were bodies. Dozens—hundreds—of bodies, crushed and maimed beyond recognition.

Passengers were flung free of the wreckage, still belted to their seats. Others were coated in jet fuel, their corpses still burning. Some hung from broken-off sections of the plane. Others had been flung atop cars or hurtled through shattered windows.

He'd seen his fair share of death in his life. But not like this. Never like this, not even in the warzones of Iraq and Afghanistan.

No one could've survived a crash like that. Not the passengers, and not those unfortunate souls trapped beneath the onslaught.

Lincoln was dead.

His brother was gone. For an instant, the grief rose up like a towering tsunami, so huge and all-encompassing it threatened to crush him, to pull him under then and there.

A memory seared through his mind unbidden, as clear and luminous as if it were happening right in this moment, a fragile, perfect thing surrounded by chaos and carnage.

It was their thirteenth birthday. An important milestone marking the end of childhood and the beginning of manhood. Their father had promised to take them fishing at Burton Lake ten miles across town. But their birthday dawned, and he lay on the couch in a drunken stupor, oblivious and in no condition to move, let alone drive anywhere.

Liam had been looking forward to it for weeks, months. Unlike Lincoln, Liam didn't care about the fishing part. Lincoln regularly went hunting and fishing with his best friend's family. Liam never went. He was withdrawn, a loner. Back then, he hadn't found solace in nature the way he did now.

It wasn't the trip itself but the connection that he'd craved as a boy. The one bright spot in an increasingly toxic homelife. A day where things could be different, where they might all pretend their father wasn't a monster; that he was a good father who deserved their adoration and they were good sons who didn't bitterly resent him in equal measure with their love.

The boys sat in the darkened house stinking of booze and vomit and broken promises, waiting for nothing, for the miserable day to end so they could go back to expecting little and getting less.

It was Lincoln who'd stood suddenly, a fierce scowl on his young face. "To hell with this. We're going anyway."

"What? No, we can't—"

"And why the hell not?" Lincoln grabbed the truck keys from the hook by the door and spun to Liam. The anger and disappointment gone, replaced with a wicked, mischievous grin. "I can drive us. The old man isn't ruining this birthday. Not for you. Not for us."

The fishing trip had always meant more to Liam than to Lincoln, who was already pulling away, already covertly mutinous, who always had friends and an outside life to escape to.

It was Liam who still stubbornly held onto the futile dream of a family that didn't exist. And Lincoln knew it.

They'd nearly crashed the truck twice. Lincoln was a horrible driver. By some miracle, they'd made it to the lake alive. The sun was bright in the cloudless sky, the water blue and sparkling. They set up their tackle and gear and Lincoln spent the whole day patiently showing Liam how to hook the worm, how to cast his line properly, how to reel in the fish once it was caught.

It was Lincoln who made that awful house bearable with his gregarious personality, his infectious laughter, his adamant optimism. Lincoln who drew Liam out of his moods, his loneliness and isolation. Lincoln who'd saved him.

Liam closed his eyes, blinking away the sudden stinging in his eyes. With every step, he felt his twin's absence like a hollowness in the center of his chest, like an amputated limb that pulsed with agony.

That always would.

He forced himself onward. The devastating pain would come later.

Now he had a mission. A purpose. The only thing keeping him going.

He said nothing to Jessa. Grief would only cripple her further. They had to move. He continually scanned their surroundings, searching for threats in the chaos of destruction and death.

Something low and lumpy lay directly ahead of them. For an instant, his brain told him it was two mannequins lying side by side on the sidewalk in the middle of downtown Chicago.

The woman was lying faceup and looked like her head had been scalped with a razor. The man was lying face down. He was completely naked but for a scorched belt wrapped awkwardly around his legs.

They were both unequivocally dead.

Jessa sucked in a sharp breath.

"Keep going," Liam said. "Don't look."

But it was impossible not to look.

They kept moving. Jessa coughed. Liam's eyes watered. The smoke nearly gagged him, burning the back of his throat and his eyes. He couldn't wipe his face or cover his mouth, not helping Jessa with both hands.

He carried as much of her weight as possible, acting as a crutch as she hobbled on her one good leg. Her every step caused her incredible agony. She took short, gasping breaths, but didn't cry or complain.

His heart thundered in his chest. His breath came in rapid pants, cold adrenaline surging through his veins. The terror was mind-numbing, made it hard to think straight. But he'd felt terror before. The soldier in him took over, focused on the task at hand. He scanned the road and buildings ahead of them, alert to obstacles and further dangers.

Those not injured by the driving debris and shrapnel hunched in front of the windows of cafes and shops, shivering, terrified, and in shock. Liam felt their eyes on him burning like brands. But none of them were armed. No one brandished weapons or telegraphed danger.

"Hey!" a familiar voice called. Liam looked back.

David Jenkins had stumbled out of the Dunkin Donuts shop. Blood speckled his coat and Bears scarf and matted the side of his head. His glasses were gone—a large shard of shrapnel jutting from his temple.

"Hey!" he called after them, his voice rising in panic. "Help me, please!"

But Liam didn't stop. He didn't owe a thing to David Jenkins. He owed everything to his dead brother and to his pregnant sister-in-law. She was all that mattered.

The street and sidewalks were strewn with pieces of plane wreckage—hunks of floor and ceiling, shredded seats, broken sections torn open, disgorging miles of tangled wires like guts.

A grouping of three plane seats hung half-way out of a third story window, teetering dangerously. The seats were empty. The nubby blue fabric was stained with large crimson blotches.

They passed a torn-off section of the cabin half-embedded in the façade of the building across the street, windows and seats intact, a few crumpled bodies still strapped in.

Suitcases and carry-on bags were flung about, some burst open, clothing and shoes and sunglasses and phones and toiletries hurled here and there by a raging monster. Credit cards, driver's licenses, and passports, torn wallets and family photos littered the dirty snow piled along the curb.

"Don't look," Liam said again.

But Jessa looked, just like he did.

He couldn't make himself turn away from the horror.

The second engine and a huge hunk of the tail had broken away from the fuselage and barreled down the center of the street, skidding and rolling and smashing cars and signs and streetlights, finally coming to a rest on its side a hundred yards from the main crash site.

A passenger slumped in the middle of the street, right on the center line. He was still seat-belted to the lower half of his seat. His clothes were shredded, his skin hanging in strips from his arms and his legs.

Liam and Jessa stumbled past him.

Liam gripped Jessa's waist tighter as he helped her step over a small Minnie Mouse suitcase, the kind that belonged to small girls who loved princesses and Disney.

They'd made it barely two hundred yards when a voice called out to them. "Help me...please..."

A dark-haired Asian woman in her thirties lay trapped beneath a ten-by-ten scrap of the cabin floor. Her left side was severely burned. Her right arm was three-quarters severed, barely attached to her shoulder by tendons and strings of muscle.

She moaned, barely conscious.

Liam's stomach roiled. He turned away and nearly wretched.

"My daughter..." the woman groaned.

Liam could barely look at the little girl a dozen yards away. She was curled into the fetal position, still clutching a stuffed teddy bear. Next to her lay a sparkly purple purse turned inside out.

The girl was gone. Her mother would soon follow.

Jessa looked at the girl, then turned to the woman. "Your daughter is going to be just fine. You just hold on, honey. Help is coming."

The woman nodded weakly, relieved and grateful, and closed her eyes.

Liam tugged at Jessa, but she hesitated, torn. Liam could see it in her face—the part of her that longed to help, the doctor who always jumped into the chaos first, ready to do her part, to save lives. She couldn't do that this time, and it was killing her.

"Come on," he urged her.

"I could use my scarf to stop the hemorrhaging..."

"You don't have the time, Jessa!"

She cupped her belly with her free hand, closed her eyes for a moment, and nodded.

They turned from the wreckage and hobbled north toward Michigan Avenue. Liam didn't look back. Back was destruction and devastation and death. Back was grief and loss and the remains of his shredded heart.

There was only forward.

7

J essa staggered. A low moan escaped her lips.

They'd left the crash site far behind. The screams of pain and terror faded. Liam couldn't see the smoke through the fog wreathing the tops of the skyscrapers, but he could still smell it. The caustic stench of burning jet fuel, melting plastic, and scorched flesh would haunt him forever.

The cold air grated against his nostrils, drying them out, making every breath raw and painful. His pulse thudded in his throat from the exertion.

They made their way along Michigan Avenue, passing the Art Institute of Chicago and Millennium Park. To his right, the open sky over Lake Michigan boiled with thick clouds that promised more snow.

Fog swirled so heavily, they might have been cut off from the rest of the world. It already felt like they were. Trapped in some eerie, bizarre episode of *The Twilight Zone* or *Black Mirror* where everything had been turned upside down and nothing would ever be the same again.

They were still more than a mile from the hospital.

The sidewalks were filled with milling, confused crowds that spilled into the streets. The traffic lights were all dark. Dozens of accidents jammed every street. Most of them were fender benders, but several were more serious. The few older model cars that worked couldn't move, trapped in the snarl of wrecked and broken vehicles.

Workers, staff, customers, and tourists streamed from offices, hotels, shops, and restaurants suddenly rendered powerless. Most of the buildings maintained back-up generators, but many newer generators now contained sophisticated electronic chips and would be as useless as everything else.

It felt like every citizen of Chicago and then some were assembling outside, braving the cold, hungry for answers.

Several Chicago PD officers were stationed at intersections working to calm the crowds and directing the injured to the closest hospitals. Two men were shouting at a police officer, waving their hands belligerently.

Liam scanned their faces—tense, nervous, bewildered, frustrated, upset. Some seemed to be verging on panic, but outright pandemonium hadn't broken out.

They didn't understand yet. Most people were used to everything on demand— electricity, heat, power, transportation, food, medicine. They were used to a world working just like it was supposed to. If something broke, a fix was a simple phone call or internet search away.

The idea that the world could go so wrong in a heartbeat—it was such a foreign thought that their brains couldn't—or wouldn't—comprehend it.

Not yet, anyway.

They would soon.

Likely, the criminal element would comprehend the gravity of the situation faster than the law-abiding population. They were used to adjusting to change on the fly, used to seizing the opportunity inherent in every disaster.

Liam had to make sure he and Jessa were off the streets long before then.

At least he had his pistol holstered beneath his coat. He would do whatever he had to in order to protect her.

"Liam..." Jessa mumbled. "I don't feel good..."

Liam helped her beneath an awning, physically shouldering several people out of their way, and settled her against the wall so she could rest her leg a little apart from the jostling crowds.

He paused to examine her. Her skin had an ashen, unhealthy sheen. Sweat beaded her forehead even though she was shivering. It was so cold that he could see the puff of each ragged breath.

He tugged off his right glove with his teeth. Cold needled his bare skin as he took her hand—cold and clammy—and felt her wrist with his index and middle fingers. Her pulse was thready against the pads of his fingers.

He checked the tourniquet. Blood still leaked in slow streams down her leg. They'd left a trail sprinkled with red along the snowy sidewalk behind them. At least it wasn't gushing.

The tourniquet appeared to be holding, but she'd lost so much blood already. They didn't have much time.

"I'm going into hypovolemic shock," Jessa said weakly.

They still had a mile to go, with no help in sight. With the crowds and the snow and the ice-slick ground, it had taken them nearly an hour to go the first mile. He didn't see them making it any faster.

He pulled his glove back on. "What do you need?"

She smiled wearily. "Blood plasma, platelet, and red blood cell transfusions. Intravenous crystalloids to start. A shot of epinephrine. You see any IVs lying around?"

"I don't have any of that."

"I know."

He wanted to smash the wall with his fist in frustration. "What do I do?"

"I need to lie down."

"We have to keep going."

She shook her head. "I can't, Liam. I won't make it."

He didn't doubt her word. She knew the medical aspects of the human body far more thoroughly than he did.

She cupped her belly protectively. The simple action nearly undid him.

He said, "I'll carry you."

She started to shake her head in protest, an automatic, instinctive response. She was a strong, smart, capable woman used to caring for herself and others.

Not this time.

"Not giving you a choice," he said gruffly.

He bent and scooped her awkwardly into his arms. His thighs and back strained as he lifted her and cradled her like a baby. At 5'7", large-boned and curvy even before the pregnancy, she wasn't a small woman. With her enormous belly, it felt like trying to balance a small whale in his arms while walking a tightrope encased in ice.

Jessa wrapped her arms around his neck and laid her cheek against his chest. Her whole body was trembling uncontrollably. Even through her coat and clothes, she was cold. Too cold.

One mile. During his time with the military, he'd regularly

hauled eighty pounds of gear through blistering deserts or tangled, mosquito-infested jungles. But that was before his back injury.

He was still in great shape. He could do this.

8

"Move," Liam snarled at a clump of teenagers huddled on the corner of Madison and Jackson. They stepped quickly aside.

"Jerk," a girl mumbled.

He ignored her.

He trudged on, passing Madison, Washington, and Randolph.

He considered telling everyone he passed to get home, pack up everything they could carry, and escape the city while they still could.

The generators would run out in a few days. Then what would all these people do in their freezing buildings in sub-zero temperatures? They had no fireplaces, no wood-burning stoves, no firewood.

What would they do when the food and water stopped arriving at the stores like clockwork, and they were trapped with almost three million hungry, freezing, desperate people?

At his homestead in Mayfield, just south of Traverse City and located outside of Traverse City State Forest, he didn't have much, but he had enough firewood cut to last the harshest winter. He had twelve months of supplies and woods chock full of deer, squirrels, and rabbits to hunt. His property had a well with a handpump, a wood-burning stove, a generator, and a few solar panels.

He would survive—as long as he could return safely to his homestead.

His handheld GPS wasn't working, and he hadn't had time to acquire a paper map of Chicago. While he'd waited at the terminal before his departure, he'd downloaded a map of Chicago onto his phone. Little good that would do now.

At least he had the paper map of Michigan he always kept with him. With the built-in compass on his mechanical watch, he could find his way.

He had his go-bag with forty-eight hours of emergency supplies. He had his pistol with three magazines of extra ammo and his tactical knife. He could find an older car that still worked, hot-wire it or steal the keys, and make it out of the city and home by tomorrow night.

It sounded easy enough. He knew it would be anything but.

Anxiety tangled in his gut, but he tamped it down. Those were problems for later. Right now, he had Jessa and the baby to worry about.

They crossed DuSable Bridge and began the trek up the Magnificent Mile.

Wreaths hung along the streetlamps. Christmas lights were strung from windows and wrapped around sign posts—none of them working. The decked out Christmas trees in the display windows looked garish and wrong without the warmth of twinkling yellow lights.

"Lincoln..." Jessa mumbled against his chest.

His heart jolted. A wave of grief rolled through him, threatening to take him under.

"It's Liam," he said.

"Liam...I miss my mom. I want my mom..."

"I'll get her for you. Both of your parents. Just as soon as we get to the hospital."

He glanced down at her. Her eyelids were drifting closed. Her skin was turning a sickly gray.

"Don't fall asleep on me."

She was so cold. Her pants and coat were still damp with her own blood. In addition to the shock and the blood loss, hypothermia was a concern.

He jostled her slightly, just enough to snap her out of it. "Stay awake!"

She raised her head, nodded groggily. She lifted her arm and felt her own wrist with two fingers to time her pulse. "Liam."

He didn't say anything. Kept walking. Had to place each foot carefully to keep from slipping on the wet, slushy sidewalk. The cold stung his cheeks and burned his throat with each breath.

His legs, back, and biceps ached from the strain of her weight. He longed to shift position but was afraid of dropping her. Less than half a mile. They would make it.

Up ahead, two horse-drawn carriages waited beside a tangle of wrecked cars in the middle of the intersection. The drivers and several bystanders were loading the injured into the carriages, presumably to hurry them to the nearest hospital. Both carriages were already full.

Briefly, he considered hijacking one for Jessa. She would get medical care that much faster. But the families of the wounded would only remove their loved ones at gunpoint.

49

It would take time and effort he didn't have. Plus, he'd have to put Jessa down to wield the gun. It didn't make sense.

He continued on foot.

"Liam," she said again, her voice soft but clear. "We need to stop."

"We're not stopping."

"Just for a few minutes. I'm so cold. Please."

He almost slipped on a chunk of ice but managed to regain his footing. She sucked in a pained breath.

He glanced down at her again. Snowflakes drifted from the gray haze of the sky and landed in her eyelashes. Her beautiful features were pinched with pain. Her eyes were glassy, her pupils huge.

"No more than five minutes."

Her arm loosened around his neck, her grip weakening. "Five minutes."

He stepped off the curb and wound between several cars to escape the crowds. He stood in the middle of the street, turned in a slow circle, and scanned his surroundings.

The Intercontinental stood across the street, a fancy historic hotel with light glowing from the windows. They were using a generator. They'd have soft sofas so she could rest for a few minutes. Alcohol at a bar he could use to sanitize her wounds. Maybe something warm to drink if they were lucky.

Dread and grief nipped at his heels.

Who was he kidding? Their luck was fast running out.

9

Liam avoided the gold-hued revolving doors, wrestled a side door open, and pushed inside. The décor was understated with its creamy tile floor, wood lacquer walls, and fat wooden pillars.

A giant two-story Christmas tree dominated the lobby. Green garlands were festooned everywhere.

He barely noticed, focusing on the people instead. The high-ceilinged lobby held a few dozen people, most of them gathered into tight, worried clusters.

Only two front desk agents remained behind the expansive check-in counter.

"I'm afraid this building is for guests only," one of the front desk agents said.

"We aren't accepting credit cards," said the second agent. "The computers are down. Cash only."

"She's injured."

The agent frowned slightly. "Northwestern is a half mile away."

"We're going there. We just need a minute."

Liam glanced around. The lobby was smaller than he'd thought it would be. A wide staircase led to a second floor featuring several black leather chairs. But there were no sofas, no soft carpet to lay her down.

Blood dribbled down Jessa's injured leg and spilled onto the shiny, immaculate tile floor.

A security guard with his hands loose at his sides stepped forward. "Sir, you can't stay here—"

Anger surged through his veins. Liam shifted Jessa in his arms and managed to jerk his wallet out of his back pocket. He always kept cash on him in case of emergency. He had two hundred in twenties in his wallet and several hundred in his go-bag.

He chucked his wallet at the desk agent. "Take what you need. If we're here longer than ten minutes, I'll pay more."

"That's unacceptable—" the woman sputtered.

Jessa groaned.

"We're not leaving." If they wouldn't take money, he'd have to up the ante. He didn't want to pull out the gun, but he had no patience for pretentious morons, either. "I need to lay her down somewhere."

"That will be fine," said a smartly dressed Indian woman as she came out from a door behind the counter. Her nametag read 'Prisha Hunjan, Vice President, Customer Relations.'"

"She's getting blood everywhere—"

"I'll take care of it," the Indian woman said.

The first agent shook her head with a scowl. "Fine. It's your butt on the line."

"I take full responsibility." Prisha Hunjan pressed her lips together as she took in Jessa's condition. "You don't need to worry about it."

The first agent folded her arms across her chest and shook her head. If she'd stuck her nose in the air, he wouldn't have been surprised. Just another reason why he hated people.

Prisha picked up his wallet and tucked it into the pocket of her skirt. She didn't even check inside it. She strode around the corner and gestured to him. "Come with me. She needs to lie down. She needs a bed."

He followed her without a word. She led him through a winding series of rooms he barely noticed to a bank of elevators. He carefully maneuvered Jessa inside. Prisha pushed a few buttons and the elevator soared upward. "Thank goodness for the generator."

He didn't say anything.

"We heard there's been multiple plane crashes."

He nodded. "She got hit by shrapnel."

"Is she all right?"

"No," he said. "She's not."

"I can't call an ambulance. None of our phones are working, not cell phones and not the landline phones, even with the generator."

"I know."

The elevator doors opened. Prisha led them to a room and opened it with a master key. Liam glimpsed gray carpet, white walls, and most importantly, a crisp white bed. The room was warm and the bed was soft. That was all that mattered.

Gently, he laid Jessa on top of the bed.

Prisha made for the door. She hesitated, glanced back at Jessa's swollen belly, and pursed her lips. "Can I do anything to help?"

"Towels," Jessa murmured. "Clean towels. A bowl of warm water. Something to sterilize with—rubbing alcohol."

Prisha gave a curt nod. "I'll hurry back."

He loosened his scarf, took off his gloves, and stuffed them in his pocket. The snowflakes that had gathered on his head and shoulders were melting. Wetness gathered at his forehead beneath his beanie and the back of his neck.

Liam sank onto the bed next to her, careful not to bump her. Jessa's eyes were closed. She looked almost like she was sleeping, except for the deathly pallor of her skin.

She said it so softly, he almost didn't hear her. "He's dead, isn't he?"

He couldn't ignore it—or her insistent questions—any longer. He leaned in close. Licked his lips, swallowed. Forced himself to speak the words. "Lincoln is...yes. He's dead."

The skin around her eyes twitched. Her lower lip trembled. But she didn't collapse into tears or break down. She already knew, he realized with a start.

"You lied to me," she said evenly, every word spoken with great effort.

He didn't apologize. "You needed to focus on surviving."

"You left him." She opened her eyes and looked straight at him.

"I—I had to." He forced himself to meet her accusing gaze.

"To save me."

It felt like all the oxygen had been sucked out of the room. Liam opened his mouth, but nothing came out.

The truth was that he *had* saved Jessa because of his brother. But also, because Liam loved her. Had always loved her, from the first day they'd met.

"Yes," he said finally.

10

Liam's mind flashed back to the moment he'd met her and lost her, all in the same night.

They had attended some stupid college party, him and Lincoln. They weren't in college but had friends who were. They were both about to ship out on their first tour in Afghanistan.

Lincoln loved parties; Liam hated them. He went for his twin, like he always did.

He'd quickly escaped the chaos to the peace and quiet of the deck. She was there, leaning against the railing in a wine-red sundress that matched her lipstick, her black braids tucked over her bare shoulders, the setting sun turning her light brown skin a burnished bronze.

She held out a sweating root beer. *Escaping all the crazy extroverts?* She'd said with that grin that melted his insides from the very first time she'd bestowed it upon him.

They'd talked and laughed so easily—and conversation never came easy for him. He was the quiet one, the outsider, the guy who never fit in, who could never quite relax or let down his guard.

In less than thirty minutes, he'd fallen completely under her spell.

After she'd gone back inside, he'd spent another thirty minutes trying to figure out how to ask the girl of his dreams on a date.

She disappeared until later that night, well after midnight, but the party was still going strong. Normally, he left a party as soon as he could. But not this one. Not until he talked to her again.

Someone put on U2's "With or Without You", a song he'd always loved. And then there she was, in the center of the living room with the couches and end tables all pushed back against the wall, with her wine-red dress swirling around her thighs, her head flung back, her braids whirling, that radiant smile lighting up her face, lighting up the entire night.

He elbowed Lincoln. "See that girl?"

Lincoln's eyes brightened. He nodded enthusiastically.

Liam said, "Think I'm gonna ask her to dance."

"Good call, brother!" Lincoln shoved his red Solo cup into Liam's hand, beer sloshing over the rim. "I'm going in. Wish me luck!"

Maybe it was so noisy that night that Lincoln didn't hear him correctly. Or maybe it was just so out of character for Liam that Lincoln brushed his crush off as inconsequential.

It was Lincoln who asked Jessa to dance. Lincoln who dazzled her with his humor and charm. Lincoln who got her to fall in love with him.

Maybe at first, she'd thought Lincoln was Liam from the deck. He'd always wondered. But after that night, it hadn't mattered. Her heart belonged to Lincoln. And his heart belonged to her.

Their whole history passed in front of his eyes in a heartbeat.

How hard it was to be around them. How easy it was to make excuses not to visit, to drift apart, to nurse his loneliness in private, to tell himself it was safer and easier for everyone if he just stayed away.

Not only from his brother and his wife, but from life in general.

Regret filled him, so bitter he tasted it like ashes on his tongue. What a fool he'd been. And still was.

"If I hadn't left him," he said to Jessa, "he would've hated me forever. He would pick you to live a thousand times out of a thousand. I had no choice."

He half-expected her to yell, to rail at him, to hate him for killing her husband, for letting his brother die. He tensed, waiting for it.

But she didn't. Her chin dipped in the slightest acknowledgment.

Maybe she would've hated him if she hadn't been pregnant. The baby changed everything. She understood he'd saved the life she carried just as much as he'd saved her. Or maybe that's how she chose to see it, because that's what she would have done in his place.

The truth was far messier than that. He loved them both. He'd resented them both, too.

His heart clenched with grief, regret, and remorse.

"Liam." She squeezed his hand with weak, cold fingers. Her eyes were wet, but she didn't cry. She was gathering the last of her strength for a different battle. "I need you to listen to me. I need you to really listen."

He stared at her.

"My parents' apartment. It's less than four miles from here, in Lincoln Park...I'll give you the address. I need you to memorize it."

"I told you. I'll get them after you're safe."

"It's too late for that."

"We need to go. The hospital—"

"I'm not going to make it to the hospital alive."

He reeled, stunned by her words.

She took in a labored breath. "My heart is racing. It's trying to keep up circulation, but it isn't pumping enough blood to my body. My brain...the confusion...I don't have much time. I'm developing ischemic injury of the vital organs, leading to multi-system organ failure. I'm—I'm dying."

"Then why aren't we—"

"It's too late for me." Her hand pressed to her lower belly. "It's not too late for him."

He rocked back on his heels, too dazed to comprehend her words. "You're not going to die. I won't let you."

Her lips pressed together. "I need you to listen carefully...to my instructions. There's not much time...okay?"

He nodded numbly.

"He's likely already losing oxygen. The best outcomes in terms of infant neurologic status occur if the infant is delivered within five minutes of maternal cardiac arrest."

"I don't know what that means."

"He's going to live, Liam. You're going to make sure he lives."

"How?"

Her eyelids fluttered. Her breathing was shallow—too shallow. "By cutting him out of me."

11

___

L iam listened to every word Jessa spoke, dread and fear and grief churning in his gut. He didn't want to do this. He'd rather be anywhere on the planet than here.

Her voice grew weaker as she gave him instructions. He committed them to memory, his gaze pinned on her face, his heart jackhammering, everything in him screaming *no, no, no!*

"Fight it!" he begged her. "Stay with me. I'll pick you up right now and I'll run. I'll get you there. I can get you there."

But she wouldn't fight. She couldn't fight. Her body was giving up on her, and she knew it. She accepted her fate. Her only thoughts now were to protect the son who depended on her body for nourishment, for oxygen, for life.

"Five minutes," she whispered.

And then she let go.

"I love you," he said. "I'll always love you."

Her eyelids fluttered and went still. The hand he'd been clutching so tightly went limp.

He stared desperately at her face, at her eyes, searching for signs of life, for *Jessa*. Unable to move, to even breathe. His pulse roaring in his ears.

His heart ripping apart with every passing second.

He leaned in close, held his hand over her nose, hoping for a puff of breath, for anything. He was so close he could smell the jasmine of her perfume, could count her lashes, could see the faintest beauty mark in the center of her chin. So close he could have kissed her.

But he couldn't. Not now, not ever.

Her face was flat. Her eyes empty. She couldn't see him anymore. She couldn't hear him anymore.

The woman he loved was gone.

He sank back on his heels, eyes wet and stinging, utterly devastated. Sorrow and grief clawed at his chest. He felt gutted. His insides were being torn out with rusted razor blades.

In less than an hour, he'd lost everything that mattered to him.

"Oh, no." Prisha stood in the doorway behind him. She'd brought a cleaning cart holding the towels, bowl of water, and a first aid kit. "Is she? Has she...?"

Liam closed his eyes and opened them to the same damn world Jessa had just left.

A world he'd had little use for before the EMP and had even less use for now.

"She's dead," he said dully.

Prisha covered her mouth with both hands. "The baby. The poor baby."

He blinked again, stared at Jessa's round belly. *The baby.* Lincoln's baby. He was still alive in there. Jessa had begged him to save her child with her last breath.

What the hell was he doing?

Adrenaline surged through him. He forced himself to get

ahold of himself, to focus. The world could go to hell, but not yet. Not until he'd fulfilled his promise.

He leapt to his feet, shucked off his coat, and pulled out his tactical knife. It wasn't a scalpel, but he kept it honed and sharp as a razor. It would do.

He glanced at his watch. 11:55 a.m. He had less than five minutes.

"You wanted to help?" he said. "I need to sterilize this blade."

She handed him the bottle of alcohol, and he poured it over the blade. Sterilizing it didn't matter for Jessa anymore, but he was worried about accidentally cutting the baby.

He was terrified he'd mess up. More terrified his fear would cause him to hesitate, to waste precious seconds, and he would lose the baby altogether.

Prisha watched silently as he repositioned Jessa's body on the bed so he could reach her belly and see clearly what he needed to do. Her maternity jeans had no zipper or snap, just a wide band of blue cloth with elastic at the top.

He pulled her pants down over her hips, then spread a towel across her crotch to give her privacy. It didn't matter that she was dead. She was still Jessa to him. She still deserved respect.

Jessa had instructed him to cut low at the pubic line to avoid harming the baby. Carefully, he cut a line through the skin tissue like a smile ending below each hipbone. The skin separated, exposing a thin layer of whitish, marble of fat. Blood oozed, but far less than he'd thought.

The blade hit resistance at the abdominal muscle. He was scared to press too hard. He sliced tentatively. It wasn't enough. The muscle was harder and tougher than he'd thought.

It's not Jessa. You're not doing this to Jessa.

He gripped the knife, slick in his hand, and steadied his other hand on her stomach. Both hands were smeared with blood. He cut again, more firmly this time. The muscle sliced open.

He dropped the knife and placed both hands inside the cut. He tugged and pulled at the warm, wet, squishy insides of the human body, pushing aside a few slick ropy intestines, his fingers searching, searching for the uterus.

He pushed further in and felt something move against his seeking hands. The baby. Tiny feet or arms poking against the walls of the uterus.

He didn't have the time to glance at his watch, which was too bloody to see anyway. How much time had passed? Three minutes? More?

He felt the seconds slipping by. Every second, a second Jessa and Lincoln's child went without precious oxygen. He held his breath along with the baby.

He picked the knife back up, tried to push the baby out of the way with one hand, and made a long, shallow cut with the other.

A gush of fluid spilled over his hands. His heart stopped beating. Was it blood? What had he just done? Had he cut the baby? Had he accidentally killed him?

But no. The fluid was clear. Not blood.

Amniotic fluid from the amniotic sac. Jessa had warned him. In his fear, he'd forgotten.

There was so much gushing out, he couldn't see anything clearly. He grabbed a towel with one hand and daubed it over the cut, mopping up as much of it as he could, just enough to see what he was doing.

He couldn't afford to cut too deep or too hard, especially with the amniotic fluid obscuring his view. The rest he would do with his bare hands.

He shoved his fingers into the laceration and tugged. He pulled harder—nothing wanted to come out.

The human body resisted being pulled apart, even in death.

His mind revolted from the actions of his body, revulsion and fear roiling in his belly. It was gruesome and barbaric. He nearly vomited.

How many minutes had passed? Four? Already five? His blood rushed in his ears with a dull roar. Prisha said something but he didn't hear her.

With a ferocious grunt, he pushed both hands inside. He felt tiny slippery feet, buttocks, and a thin torso. So small. So achingly fragile.

What now? He couldn't just yank the baby out in case he tore or broke something crucial. But he had to move fast. His heart pounded, his lungs burning for want of oxygen. How much worse was it for the baby?

The baby will be head down, Jessa's voice said inside his head. *Slip your hand underneath him.*

He obeyed. His big hand slid beneath the baby's body. With his other hand, he grabbed the shoulders with his fingers splayed along his back.

Liam plucked the infant out of his dead mother's womb into the bright and angry world.

12

L iam inhaled sharply, precious oxygen flooding his system.
The infant lay in his hands, impossibly small, one tiny
fist smaller than his thumb. His little feet kicked weakly. He was
bluish, wrinkled, and covered in red blood and whitish goop.

He was moving, but he wasn't making a sound.

Liam's gut lurched. Was the baby breathing? He couldn't tell.

He didn't know. He didn't know a damn thing.

Jessa's words echoed in his head again. *Rub his sternum gently
to stimulate breathing.*

He grabbed one of the white hotel towels and wrapped the
baby inside it, careful to keep his face free. He cradled him in one
arm and rubbed his chest with two fingers.

"Breathe, damn it, breathe!"

The infant opened his mouth and released a tiny, scratchy
wail. His chest rose and fell.

He was breathing.

Liam let out his own relieved breath. He examined the child's arms and legs, counted the toes, checked his back and chest, ran his fingers over his slick wet scalp, the fuzzy ears, the delicate scrunched face.

Everything was present and accounted for. No lacerations or bruises.

His nephew was born perfect.

Prisha came to the bed. Tears streamed down her cheeks. She wiped her face with the back of her arm and sniffed. "Don't forget the umbilical cord."

He'd almost forgotten she was there.

She held out her hands, and he placed the child in her arms. He took the knife and hesitated, staring numbly at the strange purplish rope connecting the baby to his dead mother.

"It needs to be tied off before being cut," Prisha said. "I remember the doctors doing that with each of my own babies. Tie it between the baby and the cut. I'm not sure what to use..."

"I have something in my pack." Liam cleaned his hands enough to grab a coil of paracord from the side pocket of his go-bag. He cut an eighteen-inch length and quickly knotted it around the umbilical cord, then used the knife to cut the cord a few inches beyond the knot.

His hands were shaking. Now that the child was safe, the adrenaline dump hit him hard.

Prisha knelt beside him and together they gently rubbed the newborn until he was clean and dry. His skin shone a light cinnamon brown. The hair that had been matted to his scalp was thick, black, and curly, already almost an inch long.

Prisha wrapped him neatly in a soft clean towel and handed him to Liam. "Newborns are so fragile. Be careful to support his neck and head."

He stared at the tiny being in his arms, hardly daring to believe that it was real, that he'd done it. This terrible day had seen so much death and destruction. But here in his arms was raw and beautiful life.

It was almost too much to bear.

Prisha brought him a hand towel and the bowl of water to wash his hands clean. She hovered behind him. "What are you going to do now?"

"Hospital, I guess. Babies should be checked out by doctors."

"It's freezing outside and getting colder by the minute."

He shrugged to belie the anxiety needling him. "Don't have a choice."

She eyed him and the baby, frowning. "You should carry him inside your coat, against your body for warmth. You need a carrier, so you have at least one hand free in case you slip and fall with all that snow and ice out there."

He also needed his hands free for security. He needed to be able to get to his weapons quickly. He couldn't do that with a baby in his arms.

He mentally sorted through the items in his go-bag for possibilities. "I have paracord and an emergency thermal mylar survival blanket."

"That will help. And he'll need something for his head. The most heat escapes the body through the head, and that little one needs to stay warm. I have a winter hat, but it's much too large for him."

"I have something."

"Good. I can make you a wrap out of a hotel sheet. I've had four babies. Between us, we can figure this out. Let's get this done."

Her steady, matter-of-fact attitude calmed his nerves. Jessa would have liked this woman.

Prisha went to get a clean sheet. Still cradling the infant, Liam knelt beside Jessa's body. He didn't know what to say or do. He wasn't a praying man, but in that moment, he wished he was.

He wanted to destroy whatever evil had dared to take her from this world, who'd stolen his brother. To exact a painful and violent vengeance. It was what he did best.

But the enemy was unknown and invisible. There was no one to fight. Nowhere to direct his inexhaustible wrath and grief.

He bent and kissed Jessa's forehead. The warmth was already leaching from her skin.

He gingerly felt her coat with his free hand and reached into the right pocket. He pulled out the tiny knit hat he'd given her only hours earlier and tucked it over the baby's soft scalp.

Prisha returned with two king-sized sheets she'd cut into long eighteen-inch wide strips and tied together. He held the infant to his chest while she wound the thing around him in ways he didn't understand, then tied it at his back. It was snug, and the child felt secure.

He was sure the woman noticed the holstered pistol at his belt, but she didn't say anything.

They wrapped the emergency blanket around the front of him and secured it with a bit of paracord, making sure the baby's face was protected from the elements, but he could still breathe freely.

He shrugged his coat back on, ensuring the gun was hidden, and put on his hat and gloves. He slung the pack over his shoulders. The go-bag's weight was familiar and comfortable. The baby hardly weighed a thing.

His nephew made soft cooing sounds. He would need a bottle

and diapers soon. Liam hoped to make it to the hospital before then.

Get to the hospital. Get the child to safety. That was the only thought in his head, the only thought he could allow. He couldn't let anything else in, or the sorrow, anguish, and rage would undo him.

13

L iam gently covered Jessa with a sheet. He stood there for a moment, lost, confused, unsure what to do with her body.

"I'll watch over her," Prisha said. "Don't worry about that. You've got the baby to take care of."

Jessa's parents would want to know where she was, would want to come for the body. That wasn't a good idea. He knew that much. He hated the thought of leaving her like this, but right now, he needed to focus on the living.

Liam left the bloodied hotel room and headed for the lobby. Prisha followed him. Outside the bank of elevators, she handed him his wallet. It was untouched. She hadn't taken a single bill.

"I hope this power outage doesn't last too long," she said. "It's so bizarre about the cars and the plane crashes. And the phones." She shivered. "I just want to be home safe with my kids, you know?"

He hesitated. Most people didn't want to hear the truth. They weren't interested in worst-case scenarios or preparing for potential disasters. They didn't like thinking about all the ways the world could go to hell. It was too terrifying.

Prisha had helped him. She'd given them a room when no one else would. She'd stayed calm and steady. He owed her. "It's not going to get better. It's going to get much, much worse."

She crossed her arms protectively over her chest. "The TVs aren't working, but one of my coworkers got a radio working. The emergency broadcast says a weather phenomenon has temporarily affected several transformers and the cell towers, but power will be restored very soon. They told everyone to stay inside and conserve heat."

"They're lying to prevent a panic. But it won't work. Three days from now, this city will be in anarchy."

Her eyes widened.

"Power's not going to come back on for a long time, maybe years. Might be regional, or it might be the entire country."

"So, it's not a weather thing."

"No. And it's not temporary, either."

"This was done on purpose," she said slowly, understanding dawning. "A cyber-attack, like they're always talking about on the news."

"Something like that." He nodded. "No power means no heat. Few working vehicles means no food deliveries, no medical supply deliveries, no gas tanker deliveries. Water treatment plants stop working. Water stops coming from the tap. Gas stations stop pumping. Stores and pharmacies will empty out in three days. Generators will run out of gas a little after that."

She glanced up at the huge bright Christmas tree, at all the lights still on, even when they didn't need them. All that wasted electricity using up soon-to-be precious resources. "What are we going to do?"

"You got family or friends somewhere else? Outside the city?"

She bit her lower lip. "Yes, I think so."

He tugged out his wallet and handed her the two hundred in twenties he'd promised to pay for the room. A deal was a deal. Better she had it than the morons running this hotel.

"Collect any supplies you can. Use all the cash you have at any store that will take it. Get your family and get out, as soon as you can. The panic will start tonight when the heat doesn't come on, and people realize freezing to death might happen before they starve to death. Might be starting already."

She placed one hand on his arm. "Thank you."

He paused at the revolving entrance door. Outside, snow fell from the gray sky, heavier and thicker now. The stalled vehicles, streets, and sidewalks were filmed with a thin layer of white.

The temperatures were dropping toward zero and below. The wind chill from Lake Michigan would make things even worse.

The crowds had thinned. Maybe people were figuring out they needed to decide what to do, make a plan. Some would hunker down and try to wait it out. Others would try to get as many supplies from the stores and gas stations as they could.

"It's supposed to be one of the coldest nights on record," Prisha said. "Please take care of yourself and that baby."

With a curt nod, he left the warmth and light of the lobby and emerged into a city that would soon be cold, dark, and silent.

14

Liam trudged through the snow and the cold. He followed Michigan Avenue north to East Erie and turned right. He knew the general direction of the hospital from Jessa's instructions.

He didn't lower his head but remained alert, steadily scanning his surroundings, watching faces and body language, cataloguing potential threats.

When he finally reached the hospital, the line was out the door and trailing into the street, eight-to-ten people thick. Hundreds of people. Too many. Emergency tents were being erected on the snow-covered lawn. Nurses were walking the lines, triaging the injuries.

From all the car accidents, he thought dimly. And those injured but not killed by the plane crash. Multiple plane crashes, probably. Who knew how many others were unable to glide to a safe landing in a field or lake somewhere?

"How long's the wait?" he asked an elderly man in line. The

man's arm was cradled to his chest, a makeshift sling made out of a plaid long-sleeved shirt beneath his jacket.

The man coughed into the crook of his free arm and wiped at his red-rimmed eyes. "They're saying they're way past max capacity but will continue to receive patients. They said to be patient. I assume that means we'll be waitin' for a long, long time. Don't know how they expect anyone to be patient when we start freezing our hind-ends off right here in the street."

It would be hours before he could get the baby seen. A seemingly healthy child wasn't a priority today, not by a long shot. Even with the thermal blanket, the knit hat, and Liam's own warmth, he didn't want to gamble the life of a newborn in this biting cold.

He lifted the edge of the thermal blanket and glanced down. The infant's eyes were closed. His breathing came in small rapid puffs. His skin color still looked good.

Maybe he didn't need the hospital. Maybe it was more dangerous to wait out here and expose him to the elements.

Jessa's parents. Mr. and Mrs. Brooks. They would take the baby in. He was planning to take the child to them after the hospital anyway.

He just needed to get there. He knew the general direction of Lincoln Park, and Jessa had told him what street to look for. He checked the compass on his watch to orient himself and started walking.

His whole body ached. From the accident, from the cold, from the black despair sucking at his soul. Just get there. That was all that mattered.

A shout drew his attention. At the corner, a man in a white lab coat stood outside a CVS pharmacy arguing with two large, burly men and a woman. The woman was shouting and jabbing at his chest. "We have a prescription! We need those antibiotics for our child!"

"The computers are down. The prescription was sent electronically by your physician. I can't verify it without the computer. I'm sorry. Come back tomorrow."

"You and I both know that computer won't be up tomorrow! You're trying to hog all these medications for yourself, aren't you? You think they're gonna become real valuable real soon, and you're gonna get rich trading off other people's desperation!"

"You're being unreasonable and paranoid! Don't make me call the cops," the pharmacist said nervously.

"With what phone?" one of the big men scoffed. "Nothing works, asshole!"

"Now wait just a minute—"

Liam crossed the street, weaving between the stalled and abandoned vehicles, and walked faster. The last thing he needed was to get involved.

People were starting to get it. It wouldn't be long before similar altercations were taking place all over the city. Many would end in violence.

Block after block, lines were forming at pharmacies, gas stations, and convenience stores. At the gas stations, lines were at a standstill. The pumps were all electronic and non-functioning.

He watched a group of people stalk out of an organic foods store, pushing past those still in line, muttering angrily at the cash-only signs taped to the door.

Most people relied on their credit cards. Very few carried cash with them anymore. The banks and ATMs were already closed. There was no way to get cash unless you already had an emergency stash.

He kept moving, stopping for nothing. He tried to blend in, to keep from drawing attention to himself, all too aware of the five hundred dollars in twenties and fifties hidden at the bottom of his pack.

He stayed along Lakeshore Drive, skirting the lake and enduring the wind. Two hours later, as the day turned into late afternoon, he found the correct street.

No one was outside. The road was empty but for a few stalled vehicles. The sounds of the city had gone completely silent. The cold air seared his throat and stung his nostrils with every breath.

With the strange fog and the snow, he could barely see more than a few hundred yards ahead of him. The snow had a dampening effect, transforming the quiet into something eerie and almost otherworldly.

He located the correct apartment. It was a nice high-rise built of gray brick and surrounded by a wrought-iron fence. He strode up the walkway. His boot scraped on ice covering the bottom stair leading to the entrance.

He slipped. His arms flailed, his feet slid out from beneath him, and he landed hard on his back. Pain spiked up his spine. For a second he lay there, the wind knocked out of him, wet cold leaking into his legs through his jeans.

The baby started crying, a high, stricken wail that pierced the eerie silence.

"Sorry," he muttered.

He clambered gracelessly to his feet. A bit of snow had gotten beneath the neck of his coat. He shivered and turned up the collar.

The infant whimpered. Liam patted his head awkwardly and shushed him. Miraculously, it seemed to work. The child quieted.

He took the steps more carefully and knocked on the entrance door. No one answered.

For a desperate moment, Liam entertained the anxiety-filled possibility that he would be responsible for keeping this child alive —a responsibility that he would surely fail.

He knew nothing about children. Even less about babies.

He longed to return to the isolation of his homestead and sit out on the porch with his telescope, a rifle across his knees, studying the stars and tuning out all the chaos and misery and cruelty of a world he wanted nothing to do with.

He was meant to be alone. He survived alone. One day with other people, and he'd lost everything that had ever mattered.

Now there was just this final task before him, the task he owed the brother he should've died for and the woman he'd loved but could never have.

No one came to the door. He checked the knob. It was unlocked. Someone had left it that way or the electronic security system had malfunctioned. No bellman or security guard greeted him as he entered the lobby.

The overhead lights were off, but dim emergency lighting lined the floors. Whoever managed this building was smart. They were already conserving their power usage.

He bypassed the elevators and took the stairs. He exited on the fourth floor and found the correct number—412. He banged on the door with his gloved fist.

Be here. Please be here.

Movement behind the door. A muted shuffling sound, and the door opened a crack. Someone gasped in recognition. The door opened wider.

15

An attractive black woman in her early sixties stood in the doorway, dressed in sleek navy slacks and a lavender cashmere sweater. Her graying hair was stylishly bobbed at her chin, her makeup chic and tasteful.

She took him in, her eyes widening with surprise—and relief. "Lincoln! Oh, I'm so glad you're here. We've been worried sick. We've—"

Liam shook his head, his heart clenched like a fist in his chest. "Not Lincoln. His brother. I'm Liam."

Her brow knit in confusion, then cleared as she understood. Her gaze flitted beyond him, searching for the people she really wanted to see: her son-in-law and her daughter.

Her husband came up behind her. He was slim, his short hair and beard mostly gray, his eyes kind and lined with faint wrinkles as he smiled. "Welcome, Liam. It's wonderful to see you again. Are Jessa and Lincoln okay?"

"They're not coming." He inhaled sharply, forced down the pain. "They're both dead."

Mrs. Brooks took a step back. Her hands fluttered to her throat. "What? No. That can't be true. I talked to her on the phone this morning, before the phones stopped working. We were going to dinner...for Christmas Eve..."

"A plane crashed near Sears Tower. More than one. It—it took them both."

Mrs. Brooks' hands lowered to her chest, like she didn't know what to do with them, like they didn't belong to her anymore. They curled into fists over her heart.

She stared at Liam, shaking her head back and forth, faster and faster. "No. No. NO!"

"I'm sorry—"

"Tell him it's not true!" She looked up at her husband, beseeching him, begging him for an alternate reality that hadn't just been ripped apart, where she hadn't just lost her only child.

His eyes met Liam's over his wife's head—questioning, disbelieving, full of dread and fear. The man saw it in Liam's face—he recognized the truth. His features contorted as the impact of it struck him like a blow.

"I'm sorry, honey. I'm so sorry," he murmured, like he was somehow to blame, like he could've single-handedly prevented this disaster if only he'd tried hard enough.

Mrs. Brooks curled in on herself like a bird with broken wings, her expression stricken. She collapsed slowly, her legs giving out on her as she fell back into her husband. Mr. Brooks wrapped his arms around his wife. "No," she said again, a whisper this time, a desperate plea.

It was too much for Liam to take. He couldn't handle his own grief, let alone theirs. Everything in him wanted to turn tail and flee. He didn't. He couldn't.

Mr. Brooks looked at him, his eyes hollowed, shoulders

hunched and defeated. He looked like he'd aged thirty years in an instant.

"My daughter...where..." He swallowed. "Where is her body? We want to get her. I need to bring her home."

Liam wasn't a liar. But he lied now. If Jessa's father was anything like him, it'd tear him to pieces to leave her behind, to not honor her body the way she deserved. The man's loyalties and attention would be divided between the living and the dead—and he needed to focus on the living now.

Jessa's parents didn't yet understand what had just happened to the country that they thought they knew. They were still thinking in terms of funerals, coffins, flowers and hymns and mourners dressed in black. They weren't thinking about the mayhem about to descend on their city, the desperation and lawlessness.

"She's gone," he said, forcing out the words. "Her body is gone. There's nothing left to go back for."

Something collapsed in the man's face—a grief too huge to quantify. Mr. Brooks had raised his daughter, his only child—changed her diapers, taught her to drive, loved and adored her. In an instant, it was all gone. She was gone, and his entire life with it.

The agonizing pain in his eyes reflected Liam's own breaking heart. He could hardly bear it.

He'd faced war. He'd faced death and destruction, faced the loss of the two people he'd loved most torn from him like his own beating heart. He would face this, too, with his head held high—even if it killed him. "There's more."

Before he could change his mind, Liam unzipped his coat and tugged down the thermal blanket. The small dark-haired head appeared. A fragile cry echoed in the dim corridor.

Mrs. Brooks gasped. She twisted around in her husband's

arms to face Liam, her blood-shot eyes widening in disbelief—and impossible hope. "The baby. He's—he's alive?"

He didn't want to tell them how everything had all gone to hell. They had enough to deal with. Images of the plummeting plane, the careening wreckage, the dead bodies everywhere flashed through his head. Jessa on the bed, blood everywhere, her eyes going dim, everything fading.

He blinked the awful memories away. They would haunt him for the rest of his life. Her parents didn't need to carry such a burden. "Your daughter—she made sure that he would be okay. She made sure of it."

Mrs. Brooks nodded tremulously. Tears streamed down her cheeks. She didn't take her eyes off the infant. To her credit, she didn't reach for him or try to pry him from Liam, though she clearly wanted nothing more in this world than to hold this child in her arms.

Liam unwound the makeshift baby carrier, carefully supported the baby's back and neck, and held out the newborn. Forcing his arms to move was the hardest thing he'd ever done. This was his nephew. His brother's child. He already loved this child with every beat of his heart.

Jessa's mother took the baby with gentle, trembling hands. She cradled him to her chest, touched the tiny balled fists, ran her fingers through the thick dark hair.

Liam's hands fell to his sides, empty.

She wept openly. So did her husband. They both cried tears of grief mingled with joy. Their lives had been shattered and remade again in the space of heartbeats. They had a purpose now, a piece of their daughter still alive through the gift of their grandson.

"Thank you, Liam," Mr. Brooks said gruffly. "I can't tell you—you'll never know how much this means to us."

He did know. He knew how hard it was to hand Jessa's child over, how an immense pressure crushed his chest until he could hardly breathe, how he was left utterly bereft.

"You—you brought our heart back to us," Mrs. Brooks said. She looked so much like her daughter. He saw it in the regal structure of her features, her proud chin, the warmth of her eyes, the full, wide mouth that trembled now, but would light up a room when she smiled.

"He needs food and diapers," Liam said, because if he didn't focus on what needed to be done, if he didn't concentrate on what happened next, he would fall apart right here on their doorstep.

"We—we have formula. And bottles. And diapers. I was going to watch him when Jessa went back to work. I was so excited, I bought everything we'd need early..." Her face contorted again as she fought back another wave of grief.

Grief warred with hope. Hope won. He saw it in her face, in the determined line of her shoulders as she mentally prepared herself for the challenges ahead. Her arms tightened protectively around the baby.

Something released inside his chest, a breath he hadn't realized he'd been holding. His nephew would be cared for here, with them. He would be loved and cherished. A child couldn't ask for more than that.

In the end, that was the only thing that mattered.

"Come inside." Mr. Brooks gestured to Liam. "Please. Stay with us until the power comes back on. It's vicious out here. You've—you lost them, too. Stay with us."

He couldn't stay. He was an outsider here. He didn't belong.

He cleared his throat, swallowing hard. "I have other plans. I'm getting out of the city. So should you."

He repeated everything he'd said to Prisha.

They nodded, faces grave. They believed him.

"We have cash set aside," Mrs. Brooks said. "And we have somewhere to go. My aunt lives in Tuscola, a tiny Amish town in Douglas County. She's got a huge rambling farmhouse. She'll take us in."

"What about a vehicle?"

"I have a 1970 Ford Mustang Boss 302 stored in the parking garage around the corner. I went to check it when my BMW wouldn't start. It still works, and it has a full tank."

There would be a lot of stalled cars on the road between here and there. But they would make it. He believed they would make it. "Good. Pack everything up and leave."

"Liam," Jessa's mother said as he turned to leave. "What is his name?"

"Jessa, she—she never had a chance to tell me. I guess that's up to you now."

Mrs. Brooks nodded to herself, her jaw set.

He started to walk away.

"I know what you did, what you must have had to do to save him..." she said from behind him. "I know this child is in our arms because of you."

He went still.

She took a sharp, unsteady breath. "Liam. His name is Liam."

16

Liam didn't turn around. He couldn't.

Couldn't let them see the wetness gathering at the corners of his eyes or the anguish twisting his features. Couldn't let them see the already-broken shards of his heart shattering into a million tiny pieces.

He put one step in front of the other and strode down the dim hallway on numb legs.

It was for the best. This was a good thing. The right thing.

Lincoln and Jessa's child was in good hands. They could care for him in a way Liam never could. They would love him like a child needed to be loved. If they made it out of the city, they could make it. He told himself they would make it.

He still felt like a giant hand had reached in and torn a wide-open hole where his heart resided. He was nothing but broken and jagged pieces, nothing but empty spaces.

It was all he could do to keep moving. It was the only thing he had left, the only direction he could go was forward or he might just collapse right there and never rise again.

He entered the stairwell, took the stairs to the lobby, and left the way he'd come, making sure the entrance door locked behind him. The wind picked up and blew snow like shards of ice into his face. He shuffled down the ice-crusted front steps, careful not to trip again.

A smudge of color amid the sea of white at the edge of the sidewalk drew his attention. He bent and picked up the tiny knit hat. His chest wrenched painfully, his breath caught in his throat.

For a moment, he considered whether to take it back up into the quiet building to Jessa's parents' front door. It was little Liam's, not his.

Instead, he brushed off the snow and slipped it gently into his pocket. He would keep it. More than that, he needed to keep it.

It was all he had left of his family.

Liam shrugged off his pack, took out a water bottle, a granola bar, and his paper map of Michigan, and rezipped it. Studying the map, he fixed his plan in his mind's eye.

Get out of downtown, then the suburbs. Skirt the lake and journey into Michigan, hugging the coast and heading north through dozens of small towns, avoiding Grand Rapids, Kalamazoo, and all the cities that would devolve into chaos, mayhem, and death within days.

With the pack on his shoulders and his beanie shoved low over his forehead, he set a determined, steady stride and headed south.

Three hundred hard miles stood between him and his destination.

He couldn't call his small, solitary house "home." He hadn't known anything like home for a long, long time. But there was nowhere else to go, nothing else he cared for in the whole doomed world. Except for the child in the arms of strangers, but he didn't belong there, didn't belong anywhere.

He was unmoored, untethered. Haunted. A lone man in a hostile landscape where everything—even nature, maybe even his own bitter soul—wanted him dead.

It would be a long journey back.

The End

ALSO BY KYLA STONE

Last Sanctuary: The Complete Series Box Set

No Safe Haven (A post-apocalyptic stand-alone novel):

No Safe Haven

Historical Fantasy:

Labyrinth of Shadows

Contemporary YA:

Beneath the Skin

Before You Break

Non-fiction:

Real Solutions for Adult Acne

ACKNOWLEDGMENTS

Thank you as always to my awesome beta readers. Your thoughtful critiques and enthusiasm are invaluable. This book especially was difficult to write, but your support and encouragement meant everything to me

Thank you so much to Fred Oelrich, Dave Farris, Carol Butz, Melva Metivier, Wmh Cheryl, Becca Cross, and to George Hall for his keen eye and military expertise.

Huge appreciation to Dr. Prouty for his medical expertise. Liam's harrowing emergency C-section wouldn't have been nearly as intense or realistic without his help.

To Michelle Browne for her skills as a great line editor.

And a special thank you to Jenny and Chris Avery for catching those last pesky errors and for lending their aviation expertise.

To my husband, who takes care of the house, the kids, and the cooking when I'm under the gun with a writing deadline. To my kids, who show me the true meaning of love every day and continually inspire me.

Acknowledgments

Thanks to God for His many blessings.

And to my loyal readers, whose support and encouragement mean everything to me. Thank you.

ABOUT THE AUTHOR

I spend my days writing apocalyptic and dystopian fiction novels, exploring all the different ways the world might end.

I love writing stories exploring how ordinary people cope with extraordinary circumstances, especially situations where the normal comforts, conveniences, and rules are stripped away.

My favorite stories to read and write deal with characters struggling with inner demons who learn to face and overcome their fears, launching their transformation into the strong, brave warrior they were meant to become.

Some of my favorite books include *The Road*, *The Passage*, *Hunger Games*, and *Ready Player One*. My favorite movies are *The Lord of the Rings* and *Gladiator*.

Give me a good story in any form and I'm happy.

Oh, and add in a cool fall evening in front of a crackling fire, nestled on the couch with a fuzzy blanket, a book in one hand and a hot mocha latte in the other (or dark chocolate!): that's my heaven.

I mean, I won't say no to hiking to mountain waterfalls, traveling to far-flung locations, or jumping out of a plane (parachute included) either.

I love to hear from my readers! Find my books and chat with me via any of the channels below:

www.Facebook.com/KylaStoneAuthor

www.Amazon.com/author/KylaStone

Email me at KylaStone@yahoo.com

Or join Kyla Stone's Reader Fan Group HERE!

SNEAK PEEK OF EDGE OF COLLAPSE

1
───────

HANNAH

DAY ONE

The light went out. That was the first thing that alerted her.
The single lightbulb encased in wire mesh on the
ceiling glared down on her continuously, twenty-four hours a day,
seven days a week, three hundred and sixty-five days a year.

The sudden darkness pressed against the backs of Hannah
Sheridan's closed eyelids. Her body sensed the change and woke
her from her restless nightmares.

She sat up on the bare mattress on the cold cement floor. She
turned her head left and right, straining her eyes.

At first, she thought she'd been plunged into complete and
utter blackness.

But no, the narrow rectangle of window on the southwest side
of the room allowed in the barest trickle of dim light. The window
was located beneath the back deck. Very little daylight made its
way to her down here, filtering through the iron bars.

She'd grown used to it.

Hannah blinked, let her eyes adjust.

Shadowy shapes appeared—the bean bag in the corner, the

doorless bathroom across from her, the small fridge, the rolling cart with the microwave, the narrow counter with the sink and the cabinet where she kept her dishes along the far wall.

The silence.

That was the second thing.

She was used to quiet. But this was something else.

The rumble of the generator outside the window. The buzz of the small fridge. The cycling of air from the heating and air conditioning unit.

Everything had gone still and silent.

No sound but her own breathing. In and out. In and out.

For several long minutes, she didn't move.

Was this another trick? A trap just waiting to spring its jaws?

She was used to tricks, too. She lived inside a trap.

The light didn't come back on. The fridge didn't buzz. The generator didn't rumble back to life. She glanced at the tiny camera affixed to the ceiling above the secure metal door.

The little glowing green dot no longer glowed. The camera was blind.

The power had never gone out before. He came and checked it almost every week, made sure everything worked and remained in pristine condition—the electricity, the water, the heat, the camera, the security system.

The generator kept her alive. It also kept her trapped.

Slowly, she pushed aside her two blankets and rose from the mattress in the corner of the room. Her bare feet hit the chilly concrete floor, but she barely noticed.

Her mind spun and whirred, confused thoughts ricocheting against her skull. Nothing made sense.

Why would the power go out? Had he forgotten to refill the generator? Was it something else? A storm or a power surge?

When would it come back on? Would it come on? Would he know it was out and return to check on her?

Sometimes, he came every seven days. Sometimes, two weeks passed. There was no rhythm or reason to his visits.

No way to tell how many days she'd need to survive before he returned. If he returned.

It was easy to lose track of time here. At first, tracking the days had been of crucial importance. Counting the hours. The days, weeks, months. Then the years.

Always hoping for rescue. Praying for it. Desperate for an escape that never came.

She looked at the calendar she'd made with chalk on the wall above the mattress. It was too dim to see them, but her mind conjured the images clear as day. She'd stared at those blunt marks hundreds, thousands of times.

She knew it was day by the dull gray light. But what day? What month? November? December? Or even later? When had she stopped keeping track?

Only a few weeks. No, it was longer. Maybe even months.

Her mind was clouded and foggy, like it had been stuffed with cotton. It was hard to think straight. Got harder every day that passed, every day that took her further from who she used to be and sucked her down deeper into this hell that never ended.

Fatigue gripped her and tugged at her arms and legs. Who cared what day or month it was? Nothing ever changed. Nothing ever would.

Her entire life consisted of these four cement walls. A fifteen by twenty room.

She should've given up long ago.

She was close now. The despair like a sucking black hole, pulling at her, threatening to drag her under once and for all. A bottomless sea of darkness closing over her head, drowning her slowly, strangling the breath from her lungs.

For almost five years, she'd fought it. Every day, an hour of calisthenics to keep her muscles from atrophying. Jumping jacks. Sit ups. Squats. Every day, writing in the journal with the crayons he allowed her. Every day, mentally practicing the guitar or the piano. Composing songs in her head.

Imagining the life she would have if—when—she ever got out of this place. Imagining the life her husband and son were living right that minute. Her family and friends and co-workers—the whole wide world continuing on without her.

But the last few months, it had become harder and harder to cling to that miniscule seed of hope. Hope was the ultimate Judas. It had betrayed her hundreds, thousands of times.

In the end, it was hope that caused the most suffering.

Hannah stared across the room at the imposing metal door and the electronic key code and lock. She stared until the shadowy shape took solid form, until her eyes ached and begged her to blink. She didn't.

Her brain filled with the buzzing static of barely restrained panic. What if he wasn't coming back? What if the water turned off along with the generator? She had MREs and enough supplies for another two weeks if she rationed, but no longer.

She had a single cup, a single bowl, and two pans she could fill with water. And the small sink built into the counter—she could fill the basin.

How long would that last? A few days? A week?

What about the heater? The chilly cement floor felt like it was growing colder by the minute. Even the air on her face and hands felt cooler.

She thought she was still in Michigan, though she wasn't sure.

Wherever she was, the winters were brutal. Only the heater kept her from freezing to death down here.

She knew the season by the temperature drop, the coldness of the floor. When she pushed the rolling cart beneath the single window, climbed on top of it, and peered out through the bars, she could see the snow on the ground, sifted beneath the wide wooden planks of the back porch.

She would freeze to death long before she ran out of food or water.

Outside, the dog barked. He'd been quiet the last day or two. She'd never seen him, but she'd pictured him in her mind a million times. Judging by the deep menace in his bark, he was a huge German Shepherd/Wolfhound/Rottweiler mix, with vicious eyes and razor-sharp teeth.

A monster. Just like his owner.

Placed there like Cerberus guarding the gates of Hades in case anyone was stupid enough to try to get in—or out.

She'd never heard another human voice, other than *his*.

The man who'd put her here. The man who kept her imprisoned like a rat in a cage.

No neighbors. No visitors. Only the damn barking dog and the occasional rumble of a truck or snowmobile engine when he came to see her.

Fear crept into the corners of her mind, anxiety tangling in her belly. She padded to the center of the room and turned in a slow circle, trying to push the cobwebs from her sluggish brain, trying to *think*.

She wrapped her arms around her thin ribs and rubbed her arms. She wore a hunter green knit sweater that matched her eyes over a thin nightgown with a pair of long johns beneath them—the same clothes she wore every day, washed in the tiny sink once a week by hand.

How long would it take the temperature to drop to intolerable levels? How long for the human body to freeze to death inside an unheated concrete basement?

Maybe, it was nothing. She was panicking over nothing. The electricity would switch back on in an hour or a day. Everything would return to the horrible state of normal she'd endured for years.

Somehow, she knew it wouldn't.

Maybe he'd finally tired of her and decided to let the generator run out. Decided to let her suffer slowly, to die in degrees by starvation and freezing to death.

That thought didn't ring true. When it was time to kill her, he would do it himself. She knew that like she knew her own name.

Something had happened. He'd been killed in a crash or struck by a train or dropped by a brain aneurism. Anything was possible.

There were a thousand ways to die. A hundred ways to go missing, to suddenly disappear from your own life.

She knew that better than anyone.

As much as she longed to see him dead, he was her only link to the outside world. To life. She loathed him but depended on him for every single thing.

He'd used that to control her completely. To exert his indomitable will over every aspect of her pitiful life.

Grinning with that dead-eye smile as he keyed in the lock code each and every time he entered the room. *Hurt me and you kill any chance of ever getting out of here alive.*

He wasn't stupid. He knew how lethal hope was—how powerful a weapon it could be.

She felt the door like a physical presence to her right. Looming just at the periphery of her vision.

She turned again, faced it. The cold of the floor leached through her feet. Sent chills racing up her spine. She shivered. Nothing worked. Not the power. Not the heat. Not the little blinking camera.

What if...

She lowered her hand to her stomach, nearly touched the rounded, basketball-sized belly, but didn't. Her hands dropped limply to her sides.

The door was always locked. A power outage wouldn't change that.

Hannah Sheridan was just as trapped as she'd ever been.

2

HANNAH

DAY ONE

Almost without thinking, Hannah found herself moving numbly, mechanically toward the sink. She knew every inch of this room by heart. She didn't need to see to know what she was doing.

She pulled her two pans out of the cupboard and filled them with water. She set them on the counter. Next, she filled her single cup and bowl. She plugged the small stainless-steel basin of the sink with the stopper and began to fill it.

A few days-worth of water. She wouldn't use the water for anything but drinking, conserving as much as she could until it ran out.

But the cold...that would kill her faster than anything. She only had the two blankets and the sweater she already wore. It wouldn't be enough.

None of it would be enough.

She would die here in this horrible prison. There wasn't a damn thing she could do about it. Panic and dread swirled in her stomach. Nausea crawled up her throat, and she almost retched.

She tugged the hair tie from her wrist and pulled her thick, waist-length dark brown hair into a messy bun. She used to brush it every day. But lately...lately she could barely muster the energy to feed herself.

He made her pay for that.

He liked her pretty. He never struck her face. Never pulled out her hair.

And he liked her clean. She always had shampoo and conditioner, bodywash and deodorant, toothpaste and an electric toothbrush. He kept the cupboards and the minifridge stocked with microwavable meals, pastas and proteins and canned fruits and vegetables.

She'd learned what happened when she didn't eat, when she didn't keep herself clean and presentable.

She glanced at the door again. Locked. It was always locked.

Absently, she touched the mangled fingers of her left hand. They were permanently disfigured—broken one by one, again and again. The pain so excruciating, she'd passed out.

He'd woken her up with a pan of cold water dumped on her face, only to start with the next finger.

Disobedience brought pain. Defiance brought pain. Hope brought pain.

It was the first lesson he'd taught her.

She was stubborn. She never learned the first time.

She'd tried to use the razor used to shave her legs on him. It hadn't gone well. He was fast and strong and smart.

On her second attempt, she'd unwound the metal spiral from the notebook he'd so generously provided her. She'd waited for him to get close before lunging, striking at his eye with the wire poking from her fist.

He'd jerked away at the last second. The wire scraped a deep gouge into his cheek, drawing blood and creating a scar, but no permanent damage.

He'd broken two ribs for that.

The third time, she'd rubbed the end of a metal spoon against the rough concrete floor for hours a day for days. She'd gripped the rounded spoon end in her right hand down at her side and waited. Waited until he was close but distracted, and she gathered her strength and her courage and plunged it into his neck.

She'd missed his ceratoid artery. It hadn't gone in deep enough to incapacitate him.

He'd stomped her bare foot with his boot—breaking her big toe and spraining her ankle—and re-fractured two of her fingers. *Snap, snap.*

She couldn't walk for days, could barely move, curled on the mattress in a fog of agony. She would rather die than live like this. And if she was going to die, she was determined to take him with her.

On his next visit, he'd dropped a picture onto the mattress beside her crumpled form. A photo of her three-year-old son, Milo. In the picture, her husband Noah held him, his own face drawn with grief and worry. Noah wore his deputy's uniform and stood on the front porch of their two-story colonial house in Juniper Springs, Michigan.

She understood instantly that this photo had been taken mere days ago. That he knew her family and where they lived and could get as close as he wanted at any time.

This was a warning. A promise. The next time she tried anything, it would be the people she loved most who suffered.

She had crayons and chalk instead of pencils, plastic silverware instead of metal, clothbound notebooks instead of spiral.

Those things mattered little, though. She still had the Bix razors. She had the sharp metal edges from her canned food.

But she didn't dare to use them. He'd broken her, and he knew it.

That was the day the fight to kill her captor had died.

But not the fight to survive.

Day after day, month after month, year after year, she'd managed to wake up each day, to continue to live, to continue to hope. To believe that she would get out some day, that she would see her son again. Milo. That was the seed she held onto, the thing that kept her clinging to sanity.

Hannah was incredibly stubborn. Always had been. But she was only human. Her captivity wore her down. The isolation, the confinement. The constant, never-ending cruelty and suffering.

Every day, more and more of her sanity slipped away. During the worst times, she went away in her head for hours at a time. Blank spaces filled up by nothing.

Each time she came back, she was still here in this prison of fear and pain and misery.

Hannah stood completely still in the darkness. The sink filled and she turned off the faucet. The last of the water drip, drip, dripped.

Instinctively, almost against her will, she turned back toward the door.

The dog had stopped barking. Complete silence enveloped her. The power was off. The generator wasn't working. Nothing was working.

Hope was her worst enemy. If only she could give in. Killing herself would be a mercy. She'd thought about it a million times. Let the thoughts spin round and round inside her head. Plotting and planning.

It wouldn't be hard. Not compared to this. It was far easier to give up. Easier to resign herself to her fate—a future of dying slowly, broken bone by broken bone, or a death of her choosing. It was death either way.

And yet, it hadn't happened yet. Somehow, despite everything, she was still here.

That stubborn part of her always clinging to life, to hope. Even in the face of overwhelming evidence to the contrary.

Could she bear another crushing disappointment? Even just walking across the cement floor felt like a monumental effort. All she wanted to do was lay down and go to sleep and never wake up.

The door was locked. It was always locked.

She'd beaten her fists against that immovable steel door thousands of times, struck it until her palms bled, scraped at the frame until her fingernails broke off.

She rested her hands on her belly. Felt movement. Quickly dropped to her sides again.

She took a step forward. One, two, three. Ten steps to the door.

It's not going to open. It never does. Why do you do this to yourself?

She stood in front of it. Bounced on her heels. Fear and apprehension battling with desperation, with a crazed, terrible hope.

The cement floor was freezing now. So was the air. Goosebumps pimpled the flesh on her arms and legs. The cold entered through the soles of her feet and radiated up through her shins, her thighs, her torso. She shuddered.

This was real. This was happening. Without heat, she was dead. Hope or no hope.

She rested her right hand on the handle. Swallowed hard, battling her despair, her own disintegrating mind.

A terrible tightness gripped her chest. Her ears were ringing. Her hands were shaking.

She turned the handle.

The door swung open.

To be continued...

Read *Edge of Collapse* to continue Hannah's journey. Buy it now on Amazon.com.

Made in the USA
Monee, IL
03 January 2024

50997474R00069